Holden's Heart

SILVER SPRINGS MINI-SERIES, BOOK ONE

KELLI ANN MORGAN

inspire books

Inspire Books
A Division of Inspire Creative Services
937 West 1350 North, Clinton, Utah 84015, USA

HOLDEN'S HEART

An Inspire Book published by arrangement with the author

First Inspire Books paperback edition August, 2016

ISBN-13: 978-1-939049-30-8
ISBN-10: 193904930X

Printed in the United States of America

"So, I never heard how your meeting went with Granddad yesterday."

Olivia wrapped her arms around her bent knees. "It was good. Ian is a good man." She dropped her head and stared into the fire. "Honestly, I thought I would be coming here to finalize a business proposal that would help to further my career. My publisher is always trying to think of new ways to market me and my books and we thought this would be a great adventure that would provide a real experience for my fans. Nineteenth century living at its finest."

"And now?"

She glanced over at him, his eyes fixed intently on her. "Now…" she glanced up at the first twinkling star to appear. "Now, I think your granddad was a Godsend. This place. You."

Another breeze sent a chill down her back and she started to tremble, unsure whether or not it was only from the cold.

"Come here," Holden said quietly.

She looked over at him and he had an arm stretched out to her. She scooted back and snuggled into his warmth, enjoying the feel of him next to her and reveling in the fact that she fit perfectly beneath his arm. Like a couple of puzzle pieces.

He rubbed her shoulders and pulled her in tight against him, wrapping the edges of the blanket up and over their legs. She rested her head up against him and closed her eyes.

"They should be back anytime now," Holden said, squeezing her closer.

"What do *you* think about this whole reader's retreat idea?"

He didn't respond.

She raised her head enough that she could see his face. His eyebrows had creased together and he stared studiously into the night sky.

She returned her head to his shoulder, content to sit there in silence.

"I had a different plan for the ranch," he finally said. "I thought I had everything figured out, but when I heard about you and your reasons for visiting Silver Springs, I must admit, I was more than a little apprehensive."

"And now?" she used his own question against him.

He chuckled.

"Now," he paused and she wondered if he were just doing it for the effect. "I think that I would make a wonderful Bentley Blackwood."

PRAISE FOR THE NOVELS OF AMAZON
BESTSELLING AUTHOR

KELLI ANN MORGAN

"…a roller coaster. Action, suspense, excitement, all rolled together. What a fun experience."
—Rocky Palmer on THE OUTRIDER

"The Redbourne men are the most amazing characters in the American west!"
—Lesia Chambliss on THE IRON HORSEMAN

"…beautiful settings, sweet romance, and an adventure so intricately woven that it will keep you guessing till the end."
—Tennille Rasmussen on THE BLACKSMITH

"Twists and turns of the story line keep you on your toes as you, in a page turning search, look for what comes next.…"
—B.D. Mann on THE BOUNTY HUNTER

"It was very hard for me to go to sleep without finishing this book, it was so romantic entertaining and mystifying."
—Patricia Collins on THE RANCHER

"…an incredibly compassionate and passionate story."
—Donna Feibusch on JONAH

"Kids hungry? That's too bad! Mama can't put the book down- better find the crackers in the pantry!!"
—Jennifer Sisneros on LUCAS

"Well developed characters, romance and action. I was emotionally connected... Sit back, relax and enjoy another Deardon heart throb."
—Forever Fan on NOAH

"Highly enjoyable and very entertaining..."
—R. Miller on HOLDEN'S HEART

ACKNOWLEDGEMENTS

To Kimberly Krey for asking me to work on a contemporary western and for being my first beta reader. You ROCK!

To Rocky Palmer at RVP the Man Editing for your devoted attention to helping me make my books the best they can be.

And to my alpha reader and sounding board, Grant—your brutal honesty, constructive criticism, and encouragement are instrumental in helping me create the kinds of stories that others like to read. Thank you for your love and support. I am one lucky woman to be your wife!

To my mother,
whose unconditional love
knows no bounds.

Holden's Heart

SILVER SPRINGS MINI-SERIES, BOOK ONE

CHAPTER ONE

Silver Falls, Colorado, Present Day

Gravel crunching beneath tires put Holden Kane on edge. He looked up from his desk out the window and watched as a silver SUV made its way up the drive. He closed the book he'd been studying, put his pencil down on top of the blueprints he'd been pouring over, and pushed his glasses up on his face as he leaned back in the leather chair, putting his arms behind his head.

It was going to be a long day. A long week.

Time to face the day.

He resigned himself to the inevitable.

"She's here," Holden grumbled loudly as he stormed toward the kitchen.

It irked him that, for the next week, the Silver Springs Ranch would play host to some city slicking romance novelist from Denver. He shook his head. How could his grandfather have ever believed this would be a good idea?

Granddad had been very specific in his instructions— Holden was not to leave everything up to his brothers, but was supposed to take an active role in teaching the woman about ranch life and helping her have a positive experience.

Holden walked past the enormous frost covered window and shivered at the cold emanating from the glass. He hated leaving the comforts of his study.

"I thought we weren't expecting her until supper," Grayson, the youngest of the three Kane brothers, said through a mouthful of cold cereal.

"She's early," Holden replied with a growl.

"Well, let's go meet her," Landon, the brother just younger than him, said as he pushed himself away from the breakfast table, rubbing his hands together as if excited to see what new chaos Granddad had brought to the ranch.

One thing was for sure—life at Silver Springs was never boring. He'd missed it.

"Come on, big brother," Landon said as he clapped him on the shoulder. "Don't worry. We'll put that fancy new education of yours to work before you know it." He laughed. "Besides, how bad can it be?"

A big group of romance reading fangirls taking over the ranch? It could be bad.

Really bad.

Holden sighed. He loved his granddad, but there had to be a way to make the man see reason.

Silver Springs was a ranch—a well-respected, forward-thinking, cattle-raising ranch. At least it would be after he set his new plans in motion. Silver Springs was most definitely not suited for a dude ranch.

"I'll go get Granddad." Grayson stood up, shoveled down the last bite of his cereal before dropping the bowl in the sink, then wiped the excess from his mouth as he sauntered out the back door toward the stables.

Granddad Redbourne would be over at the SilverHawk this morning in his weekly meeting with Uncle Tad—if they weren't finished already and out mending the fence in the south pasture.

Holden would swear the old man had more energy than all

of his eleven grandsons combined. He would be happy to hear that the woman had arrived.

Fun, he'd said. *An adventure*, he'd said.

Holden rolled his eyes. He and his granddad had different definitions of fun. With a resigned sigh, he grabbed his coat from the rack and threw it over his shoulders to stave off the cool March morning air.

"Fun? Ha." He snorted. "We'll see about that."

CHAPTER TWO

Olivia Blake's nerves dangled at the edge of sanity.

Jason had gotten married this morning, and she hadn't been the one standing next to him at the altar.

She sat up taller in the cushy leather seats of her SUV, cleared her throat, and whipped one side of her long, blond curls from her shoulder—determined that she would not shed one more tear for what was not meant to be.

Business.

She nodded curtly, acknowledging her need for some distance from the single life and handsome bachelors of Denver. She would focus on business. The only relationship she needed to worry about right now was the one developing between the two fictional characters in her upcoming novel and the one with her new potential business partner—Ian Redbourne.

The distraction of being on a real honest-to-goodness working ranch and potentially partnering up with an endearing seventy-year-old rancher on a unique adventure had been just what she'd needed. No pitying glances from little old gossiping cronies. No single, attractive men being thrown in her face like meat to a lonely dog by well-meaning friends. No surprise blind dates concluding poorly with an awkward handshake or hug at the end of the night. And no creepy black roses being left at her doorstep. Just wide open spaces and fresh air. Plenty of time to think, to write, and to explore investment opportunities to market her future.

She turned down the long, dirt road she hoped led to the Silver Springs Ranch. After she'd mistakenly gone to the Silver Oak, then the Silver Creek, and then stopped just short of the Silver Canyon Ranch, she was elated to see the large wooden archway over the drive that read, Silver Springs Ranch.

She'd made it.

Finally.

Why did all of the ranches around here have to have silver in the name?

She pulled through the archway and drove down the gravel drive, slowing to admire the enormous ranch house that had appeared just over the hill. Her eyes flew open wide and she sucked in a short breath as several well-built young men flooded the lawn in front of the house.

Her heart dropped and she sunk her foot a little harder into her brakes than she'd intended, inducing a squeal muffled in gravel with more than a dozen yards still to go before pulling into the drive. Sure, she'd expected ranch hands, but the older, tough-looking, leathery ones she'd seen in a recent documentary, not the kind she always made them out to be in her books.

Boy, was she wrong. There was nothing old or leathery about these men. They definitely belonged in novels. Or movies.

Two more tall, strapping males filtered out of the large, beautiful homestead and waited at the edge of the drive. The last thing she needed right now was to be surrounded by so many good-looking cowboys.

"What is wrong with you?" she asked aloud into the empty vehicle. "You are Olivia Blake and you've got this." There was a time in the not-so-distant past that sexy cowboys would have been just the distraction she'd needed to take her mind off her own failing love life.

But now, with a deadline closing in hard and fast, Olivia needed to focus. It would have been simple if writing were the only thing on her agenda this week, but there was more to a career as a successful novelist than getting words on a page. She unwittingly glanced up into the mirror as she resumed her approach on the gravel-mixed dirt.

When she returned her focus to the road, several of the men were running toward her, waving their hands wildly. With a reluctant smile, she waved back.

THUNK!

Olivia's heart dropped as her SUV halted without warning, jutting forward at an awkward angle, tilting down to the left front corner and throwing her hard into the driver's door. Pain shot into her shoulder with the impact. She closed her eyes and bit back the word that tempted the tip of her tongue. With a deep breath, she opened her eyes, thankful she was still somewhat upright.

She shifted into reverse and stepped on the gas, but the wheels just spun and she couldn't move. With a quick click of the seatbelt, she slipped it off of her aching shoulder, shoved the gearshift into park, and scrambled up the passenger side of the vehicle—raised into the air.

Tap. Tap. Tap.

She looked up at two very handsome faces staring down at her, worry etched across their brows. They had to have been very tall to be able to see in through the window at this angle.

"Are you all right?" one of them asked through the glass. His genuine smile and easy demeanor quickly put her at ease.

Olivia nodded and quickly twisted around, reaching back to roll down the window.

"Just hang tight," the young cowboy told her, patting at the air as if to calm a frightened animal. "You drove into a pothole that has been on our list to fill for a while now. Sorry about that."

"We're going to lift the car and pull you out, so just hang

on," another one called from the front of her SUV, pointing down at the tire. His sculpted arms were scarcely concealed by his light blue button-down shirt. He rolled his sleeves up to his elbows and dropped down onto his haunches.

Olivia appreciated the man's cut physique, but *lift the car?* It wasn't like she was driving a little passenger compact. In fact, Jason used to call it *The Behemoth*. The thought of her ex-fiancé curdled in her gut, but she nodded her acknowledgment. A few of the cowhands gathered at the upended section of the car and pushed down while two others lifted in the front and dragged it sideways. In moments, the SUV had been returned to level ground.

She exhaled the breath that had caught somewhere in her throat and threw open the door, mortified when it hit the one she'd admired earlier. His dark rimmed glasses did little to mask his brilliant blue eyes.

Calm. Cool. Collected. One of her daily mantras rolled through her mind as she stepped from the car with a smile that she didn't quite feel.

"I'm so sorry. Are *you* all right?" she asked with sheepish trepidation.

He took a couple of steps backward, patted at his chest and legs, then shrugged. "No broken bones to speak of."

"I'd imagine with a build like yours, you probably didn't even feel it." Heat flooded her face. "I'm sorry. Could I make that sound any less like I'm coming onto you? Because I wasn't. Not that I wouldn't. I mean, you're certainly come-on worthy, but…Oh, fiddlesticks. My name is Olivia Blake," she said as she extended her hand.

The dimple that grooved one side of his face when the corners of his mouth turned up into something akin to a smile almost made her forget that she wanted nothing to do with men—no matter how good they looked.

"Holden. Kane." He reached out to accept her extended hand, but instead of the shock she'd expected at his touch, there was only warmth. He quickly let go, but his eyes remained fixed on hers. "Welcome."

Olivia breathed an uneasy giggle and brushed at the crumpled lines of her maxi skirt.

"Hello," she said. "Thank you. I'm not sure what I would have done had you all not been here."

The first man who'd spoken to her through the window joined them and she reached out to shake his hand as well. "Olivia," she said with a nod.

"Landon Kane, ma'am. I'm sorry if it scared you. We're happy to cover any damages."

Olivia walked up to the front of the car, bending over to inspect it. Aside from a faint two-inch scratch on her bumper she would have never even noticed, it looked unscathed.

"That won't be necessary," she said, turning back to look up at Holden. "No harm done."

Wow! This one had to be the most attractive of them all. If anything, his glasses made him that much more appealing.

She cleared her throat.

"I'm looking for Ian Redbourne. Is he around?" She glanced over the property, placing a hand up to her forehead to block the bright rays from the morning sun. The ranch was picture perfect with the classic style barn, stables, and a few other small outbuildings that laid backdrop to the enormous, yet traditional homestead. She hadn't expected a well-kept lawn with tulips already blooming in the flower beds, but it fit. Everything looked…well, perfect.

When neither of the men responded, she returned her focus to them. By their likeness, Livvy guessed the two now standing side-by-side to be brothers.

Wait. Kane? Oh, no.

"I'm sorry, do I have the wrong ranch? Again?" she asked, brushing down the front of her peasant-style shirt. "I thought this was Mr. Redbourne's ranch. This *is* Silver Springs, yes?" She should have just worn the suit. At least that way, she would seem less like a bumbling idiot and more like a professional business woman.

A flicker of light glinted in Holden's eyes and some semblance of a smile cracked the edges of his mouth, treating her to another showing of that dimple in his cheek.

Wow! she thought again. This man with the well-worn Stetson and faded blue jeans fit seamlessly into the rugged landscape surrounding her. Her fans would love him.

They would love all of these men, she thought as she glanced around at the cow hands who had started to disperse, she guessed to return to their duties about the ranch.

"Yep," Landon said as he grabbed a large, flat piece of wood leaning up against the side of the garage and placed it over the hole she'd driven into. "This is Silver Springs."

She sighed her relief—embarrassed by the highly audible sound.

Holden chuckled.

Olivia liked how his smile transformed his face.

Stop it!

"Ian is our granddad," Holden clarified. "You're in the right place." He moved to the back of her vehicle. "We weren't expecting you for a few more hours, so I'm afraid he's not here right now. Our little brother has ridden out to get him over at the SilverHawk." He tapped on the roof of the car. "Can we help you with your luggage?"

She'd been in such a hurry to get out of Denver that she'd hardly packed enough for the day, let alone for the entire week—one oversized carryall and a small suitcase she'd thrown her toiletries and cute fringed boots into.

"Thank you, but I can get it." She clicked the button on her key ring and the back door floated open.

Landon whistled. "Is this everything you brought with you? For a whole week?"

Heat flooded her cheeks again and she shrugged. "I travel light." It was more of a question than a statement.

"Impressive," Landon said with a grin. "I don't think I've ever seen a woman pack this light even for one night."

Without another word, Holden, despite her previous objections, slung the carryall over his shoulders and lifted the small travelling bag into his arms. "Let's get you settled."

As they stepped onto the porch, an old, red pickup pulled up into the yard from the opposite direction than that from which she'd come. The passenger door opened and an older man stepped spryly out. His Stetson obscured his eyes and stubble covered his chin, but there was no mistaking that laugh.

Holden paused at the door, holding it open with his foot, but she turned back to meet Mr. Redbourne at the bottom of the stairs, a wide smile breaking out across her face.

"Well, if it isn't the dynamic and enchanting Miss Olivia Blake."

The old man pulled her into the kind of hug her own grandfather used to give. It felt nice. She wondered how, after knowing the man for only a few short days, she'd felt such a kinship with him. He was already like family.

"It's good to see you, little girl," he said as he pulled back away from her.

Standing just over five-foot seven and with a few extra pounds she wished had never found her, she was anything but little, but somehow, here and now, next to him and his grandsons, she could pretend.

"If you aren't a sight for sore eyes," Mr. Redbourne continued. "How have my boys here been treatin' ya?"

Olivia looked up to see Landon leaning against the post at the bottom of the stairs with his arms folded and Holden still at the top of the porch with her bags draped across his sculpted body. She smiled at the picture, then returned her focus to their grandfather.

"The adventures have already begun. I'm afraid I managed to drive my car into a hole, but they pulled me out with nary a scratch." *A bruise maybe, but no scratches.* "They have been quite the gentlemen, and I suspect that if they are anything like their grandfather, they'll turn out to be charming and persuasive," she told him with a slight bow of her head.

"Adventures, huh? Well, look at that." Mr. Redbourne glanced over at her SUV and the large newly covered hole next to it, then looked from one grandson to the other with a raised brow.

Landon cleared his throat and scratched the back of his head.

"Miss Blake, it has been such a pleasure to meet you." He glanced over at his grandfather. "It seems I've got a pothole that needs to be filled, among my other chores, so…" he nodded and gave a short wave of his hand. "I look forward to talking to you more over dinner."

"That would be lovely. It's nice to meet you too!"

Mr. Redbourne looked back and forth between his grandsons again and then returned his gaze to her with a warm and welcoming smile. "Oh, Livvy girl, you sure do an old man's heart good." He wrapped his arm around her and together they climbed back up the stairs and walked past Holden and into the house.

When Olivia stepped inside the rustic old homestead, it was as if she had been transported back in time into one of her novels. The large, spacious great room was filled with wooden furniture. An oversized stone fireplace spanned a good section of the far wall and exposed rafters substituted a more modern ceiling. The only indications they were indeed still in the twenty-first century were several well-placed electrical outlets dispersed throughout the room and a half-dozen built-in speakers she suspected went along with whatever entertainment equipment was hidden inside the over-sized cabinets above the fireplace.

Mr. Redbourne released her and strode to the other side of the room, then spun around with his arms opened wide. "Welcome to the Blackwood Ranch," he said with a wink.

Olivia laughed with excitement. The Blackwoods were the

fictitious family she wrote about in her books. She beamed at him. Heaven help her, but it was as if the place had breathed life into her novels. She half expected the ruggedly gorgeous Bentley Blackwood to walk through the door at any time.

The smack of the door hitting against wood as it closed startled her and she turned to see Holden standing there, framed like a picture on a cover, the light filtering in around him. She bit her lip. It was all she could do to stop her jaw from dropping to the floor.

Her publicist would have a heyday with him.

Focus on the house, not the cowboy, she reminded herself. *No men.*

She walked the perimeter of the room, taking in the incredible architecture and the simple, rustic décor, stopping to admire a collection of several breathtaking photographs that had magically captured the beauty of western life—the landscapes, the people, the stories. She paused when she came to a black and white photo of a young cowboy sitting on a wooden porch railing, legs up, his arm resting on one bent knee as he gazed out over the countryside at a heavily contrasted sky, his hat shadowing his face just the right amount.

"This is you, isn't it?" She turned to look at Holden, pointing at the picture, but didn't wait for him to answer. "Who's the photographer?" She asked the question to no one in particular. "His work is…is stunning."

"Granddad?" The front door burst open where yet another strikingly good-looking man stepped inside—a cousin or brother, Olivia was unsure. "Cal is ready to foal," he said. "Uncle Tad thought you might want to be there."

"Grayson, I don't believe you've had a chance to meet our guest."

Olivia made her way back over to where Mr. Redbourne stood.

"Livvy, this is my grandson, Grayson. He's the youngest of this lot. Grayson, Miss Olivia Blake."

Grayson tipped his hat. "It's very nice to meet you, ma'am."

"Likewise." She dipped her head.

"Granddad?' Grayson said again, with a tilt of his head toward the door.

"Well, Livvy, what do you think? You think we could pass it off as the home of Theodore Blackwood?"

"It's even more incredible than I imagined it would be!" she said with awe. Truly, she'd expected a small farmhouse with a few chickens in the back and an open pasture full of cows. But this was something different. Something much more.

Mr. Redbourne chuckled. "Why don't you get settled in and I'll have the boys show you around the place. I have a meeting this morning that I'm afraid I just can't get out of, but I'll be back later on and we can catch up a bit."

"I don't know if I've told you, Mr. Redbourne, but…"

"Now, none of this Mr. Redbourne nonsense. If we're going to be partners, you might as well start calling me Ian. Or, Granddad if it suits you better." He laughed. "Everybody else does," he said with a snort, glancing over at his grandsons.

"That's because you *are* our granddad," Holden said matter-of-factly, still standing just inside the entrance holding her things.

"Ignore him." Ian swatted at the air.

"Thank you…Ian. I'm excited to discuss the details."

He leaned forward, kissed her cheek, and headed for the door with Grayson. "Holden, you take good care of this little gal. And, be nice!" he called back as he walked outside.

"Follow me." Holden disappeared through the hallway corridor, muttering something under his breath.

Olivia picked up her feet and hustled to fall in step behind him. Just past the first door on the left, Holden turned up a smaller staircase and she followed him to the second floor, admiring the paintings that lined the walls as she went.

When she reached the top, Holden had already vanished from the well-lit hallway. Skylights illuminated the open floor plan. One side of the hall had a few well-spaced doors and the other an open railing that looked down into the great room.

She made her way down the hallway until she reached a room with an open door. When she peeked inside, Holden was setting her things down on the immaculately made bed.

"There's plenty of work to do. Meet us out in the stables in fifteen." He strode toward her with purpose.

Olivia held her breath.

You've had good-looking friends before, Liv. What is your deal?

He stopped just short of her and looked down, his eyes darker in this light than before.

It took a moment before she realized that he wanted to leave the room and she blocked the exit. She darted around him and over to the bed, then turned back to face him.

"Holden? What did your grandfather mean, 'be nice?'"

"I hope you brought something more appropriate to wear," he said, avoiding her question. "I'd hate to see you get yourself all dirty in that fancy outfit of yours." He raised a brow and pulled the door shut behind him as he left.

Fancy? In what world was a maxi skirt and peasant blouse fancy? And what had gotten into him?

The room they'd prepared for her was simple, but exquisite. The red sheer curtains and thick brown bed comforter screamed of masculinity. Olivia guessed they weren't accustomed to having women around the place—though the lack of dust and clutter made her think that they might use a cleaning service.

She stood next to the bed, glancing out the window into the simple countryside for a few minutes before throwing open her suitcase. It didn't take long for her to unpack her things, but she realized that in her haste she'd neglected to bring a pair of Levi's. The only pants she had were her black yoga pants. She was sure they would be really impressed with her 'writer's uniform.'

There had to be a nice department store in Silver Falls and she made a mental note to remember to ask Holden for directions.

"Yoga pants it is," she said as she held them out in front of her. "They'll go *great* with my cute white fringe boots." She bit her lip and frowned. Better than the flip flops still tucked in the suitcase's zippered pocket. It was going to be a great day. Even if she had to fake it, she'd make it a great day.

CHAPTER THREE

Why did Olivia Blake have to be so attractive?

Admittedly, Holden had expected an old, plump, make-up-less, cat lady with fake teeth and warts. At least that's the image he'd created in his mind. But the woman who'd stepped out of that SUV this morning wasn't anything like what he'd expected. It didn't matter that her blond curls nicely complimented the smoky grey of her eyes, or that she had a smile that wouldn't quit, she was still just a fiction writer—of romance no less.

"Ugh."

Holden marched out to the stables where they'd agreed to meet, picking up a flat shovel. Mucking out stalls was not normally part of his job, but he figured it was one of the worst tasks at the ranch and therefore, there was no better place to start.

Holden had planned it out perfectly and had made a list of all the things they could do to make the whole idea of having an authentic nineteenth century ranching experience less appealing—starting with confiscating all electronic devices. He doubted any city slicker could go more than an hour or two without a cell phone.

He'd listed several of the less than desirable and menial chores that could initiate the novelist into the ranching lifestyle.

Then, they could take her out to mend fences or pair cows on horseback for a few hours at a time. He doubted the woman had ever been on a horse, let alone ridden recently and he figured extensive time in the saddle would leave her aching to get back to the city.

He hadn't spent the last four years dedicating his life to learning everything he needed to run and innovate a successful ranch, graduating top of his class with a degree in Agriculture Science, only to let his grandfather make a mockery out of Silver Springs. Out of his inheritance.

He loved his granddad, but there had to be a way to make him see reason. Hosting big groups of romance fans from the city on a constant basis would just be a worthless distraction from implementing the ideas and renovation plans he had for this place.

"Olivia Blake reporting for duty, sir!"

Holden turned around to see the beauty saluting him, her arm tucked close to her body. Her opposite arm wrapped around her. He had to hold back the chuckle that threatened as he took in her appearance. She was dressed almost completely in black. Stretchy exercise pants that hugged every curve, a short-sleeved v-neck top, and a pair of fancy white fashion boots that wouldn't last five minutes out in the stables or anywhere else on the ranch.

"This isn't the military," Holden said as he set the shovel down against one of the gates and strode over to where Olivia stood. "And you certainly don't have to call me sir."

When she smiled, a little fire started in his belly. She was beautiful. And not like the women who looked like they'd missed one too many meals, but really beautiful.

He couldn't help the twitch playing on his lips when she sucked in a quick breath as he leaned toward her, reaching up to unhook one of his old college hoodies from the rack. He knew he shouldn't take satisfaction from her small gesture, but it was nice to know the attraction was mutual.

"Thank you," she said, meeting his gaze unabashedly. She graciously took the piece of clothing from him and slipped it over her head and shoulders and down her body.

Holden liked seeing her in his clothes. It was a good look for her.

The plan. Stick to the plan.

"You look like a smart man," Olivia said with a shiver. "You must think me unprepared and silly."

Number one.

"Cell phone?" he asked with his hand extended, palm out, refusing to respond to her goading comment.

"I figured I wouldn't need it if we were going to be mucking stalls or milking cows or whatever else it is we'll be doing this morning, so I left it in my room. Would you like me to go get it?" She did a little half-turn, waiting for his response.

Smart too. And not afraid of a little hard work? If this kept up, it was going to be very difficult to get rid of her. He dropped his hand to his side.

"Are those the only shoes you brought with you?" he asked, glancing down at her feet.

Be nice, he heard his grandfather's voice in his head, but he so wanted to antagonize her—if only to gauge her reactions.

"Yes," she responded after a short pause. "I…um…I'm afraid so," she said looking away from his gaze.

He liked the pinkish color now staining her cheeks.

"What?" she asked sheepishly. "You don't think clumps of manure will look good on them?"

She laughed weakly as she lifted a foot, staring at it as she twisted it back and forth, the smile slowly fading from her face. She pulled the sweatshirt's hood up over her head, and stared at the ground.

Holden bit back a laugh.

"Maybe this wasn't such a good idea." Olivia curled her fingers into a ball and she dropped them forcibly to her sides. With a curt nod, she turned to walk away, flipping the hood back off her head. "I'll talk to Ian and we'll try it another time," she said loudly as she departed, her ponytail bouncing seductively with each step. "I'm sorry to have wasted your time." She waved.

He groaned, watching her hasty retreat, stunned by what had just happened.

Well, that was easy. Too easy.

It was exactly what he'd wanted, or so he thought, so why did he feel like such a jerk?

She'd only gotten a few steps away from the stables when he found himself going after her.

"Hold on there a minute."

What are you doing?

She kept walking.

"Miss Blake," he tried again.

Nothing.

He picked up his stride and caught up to her, placing a hand on her arm.

"Olivia!"

She stopped and turned to face him, her face flushed pink—whether from the cold or from something else, he was unsure.

"Miss Blake." He cleared his throat and pushed up his glasses. He was in new territory here, unsure what he was supposed to say. "You give up pretty easily. I took you for more of a fighter than that."

"Give up? I'm not giving up. It just isn't like me to be unprepared and I don't like—"

"Not being in control?"

She narrowed her gaze at him and he laughed. He'd guessed right.

"It's just that with Jason getting married this morning and an impatient editor pressuring me for my latest novel, I needed to get out of the city, so I neglected to take the necessary time preparing for this trip. This is supposed to be fun. To be an adventure. I shouldn't have to fight for that."

"Who's Jason?"

Her eyes widened as if regretting that she'd revealed more than she'd intended.

"Nobody." She shrugged. "Not anymore."

He nodded his understanding. Jason must be an ex. And she didn't want to talk about it. He got that. An awkward silence passed between them for longer than was comfortable.

"Granddad has it in his mind that you, Olivia Blake, are destined to change the future of this ranch. Personally, I hate change—unless…"

"Unless it is your idea," she filled in.

He narrowed his eyes at her. *Touché.*

"Well…yes, I tend to come up with a lot of good ideas and I happen to have studied innovative techniques and new machinery that will make our ranch a leader in the industry."

"I'm not sure what you are trying to say."

She was straight-forward. He liked that too.

"Frankly, I think entertaining the idea of having retreats for a bunch of romance readers at the ranch is a waste of time."

She burst out into laughter. A thick, deep belly laugh. "You think because I write romance I am somehow less than you with your fancy degree," she said with a snort of incredulity. "Tell me, Mr. Kane, have you ever actually read a romance novel?"

He wasn't sure how he'd expected her to react, but that was not it. He opened his mouth, but nothing came out.

"I didn't think so."

He'd offended her. He always said the wrong things to women, no matter how hard he tried.

"Thank you," she said with a smile, "for making this decision so much easier for me."

"I just meant, we are a ranch—not a hotel, not a sideshow. A ranch."

Olivia turned and started to walk away again, but stopped after a few short steps and whipped back around. "I get it, you know. You have your organized little world here and the idea of embracing something creative scares you."

"I'm not scared."

"Then, how dare you insinuate that my readers are a waste of time. How dare you talk down to me as if I do not understand the difference between your ranch and a sideshow. I am a business woman just as much I am a writer and I have a good head on my shoulders just like you." She took another step toward him. "I may not be an academic or a 'prodigy' in the ranching world, but there is value in being able to see a situation more than one way."

She had a point.

He cleared his throat. "I didn't mean to offend you, ma'am."

"Sure you did. You said it yourself. You have plans for this place and me being here threatens those plans. But tell me, if you wanted me to be gone so badly, why didn't you just let me leave?"

He didn't have an answer that made any sense. Their eyes locked—invisible fire shooting between them.

She broke away.

"Look, I'm a little out of sorts today," she said after a few moments of quiet. "Normally, I play quite well with others. I thought it would be a great idea to have a place where I could connect with my fans and I thought it would be good exposure for the ranch too. Obviously, I was wrong. I certainly don't want to be somewhere I'm not wanted." She folded her lips together and turned around again, heading for the house.

Holden dropped his shoulders in defeat. He hadn't even made it to number two on his list. "You don't want to break an old man's heart now, do you?" he called after her.

She stopped, one foot on the bottom step leading up to the house.

He joined her at the bottom of the stairs, reaching out a hand to touch her—but he stopped before it connected and tucked it into his pocket instead.

Silence passed between them, but as she started up the next step, he swallowed his pride.

"Stay."

She tilted her head, but did not respond.

What are you saying? The logical part of his brain—the only part he generally recognized—sent warning signals up like flares.

If she stayed, everything could change and he didn't know if he was ready for that.

"Are you saying you *want* me to stay?" she asked, turning around and leaning against the base railing.

He smiled—a genuine, intrigued smile.

"Granddad would have my hide if I didn't do everything in my power to talk you into it."

She smiled back, then pulled at the front of his old hoodie. "I didn't bring a single appropriate thing to wear. Just look at me." One of her bouncy curls had come loose from her ponytail.

"I am." Before he could think better of it, he uncharacteristically reached up, brushed the curl away from her eyes, and tucked it behind her ear. He'd never been particularly good with the ladies—not like his brothers—but he couldn't stop himself from staring at her. He liked the feel of her skin beneath his fingertips.

The color in her face deepened a shade. He liked it.

She bit her lip, meeting his stare head-on.

It may have been his undoing.

"Why don't we go on back up to the house and we can make a list of everything you want to do here. Now, and later. Then, I'll drive you into town and we can get you some work clothes and better boots."

"A list?" She was teasing him and he knew it. "I'd like that. Thank you!"

CHAPTER FOUR

Jeans and a flannel shirt. Olivia guessed it was the closest uniform for outdoor work she would get to the comfort of her own writer's attire—black comfy pants, a black t-shirt, and fuzzy socks of most any color. She glanced at the full-length mirror in the dressing room and evaluated her appearance from the front, then twisted around to judge what she could see of the back.

She certainly wasn't going to win any beauty contests, but the clothes were comfortable enough and, she hoped, warm. She took a deep breath before stepping out of the small room to where Holden sat patiently on a small white section of the couch that had been separated from the rest.

When he looked up at her, he stood, setting down the magazine he'd been holding. He missed the table completely as he didn't take his eyes off of her. Heat immediately rushed into her cheeks at his silent appraisal. It had been a long time since a man had looked at her like that.

She and Jason had dated for nearly four years and she couldn't *ever* remember him making her feel the way Holden Kane was making her feel at this very moment with nothing more than a simple glance.

"What?" she asked when he didn't say anything. She tugged lightly at the shirt where it was tucked into the low-riding waistband of the jeans. "Is it too cliché?"

"Cliché is not the word I would use." His voice cracked a little and he cleared his throat, shaking his head as if changing the direction of his thoughts. "You ready? We should probably be getting back."

Holden had traipsed with her through three clothing stores and the Bucket of Boots shop. Part of her felt guilty that she had taken him away from his work on the ranch, but another part—a bigger part—was grateful for his company and knowledge of work-appropriate western wear.

"I just need to make a quick stop before we go," Holden told her as they crossed the street toward the truck. "You can wait here," he said after placing her bags in the backseat. "I'll just be a minute."

She glanced across the boardwalk to the display behind the glass window and walked toward it to get a better look. A particularly interesting collection of wire-wrapped jewelry caught her attention. She'd dabbled for a short time in the art, but it had been a long while and she admired the time and effort put into the intricate designs by the artist.

"Excuse me, ma'am…"

Olivia turned to see a tall, handsome man with white hair dressed in jeans, a white denim button-down shirt, and a bolo tie. He looked oddly familiar.

"…but aren't you Miss Olivia Blake, the writer?"

"Guilty," she said with a smile. "I'm afraid you've got me at a disadvantage."

"Why, I'm Thaddeus C. Redbourne. But most folks just call me Tad."

"Redbourne? I thought you looked familiar. You had a horse foal this morning." She extended her hand to his, which he immediately enclosed in his grasp.

"That's right. I can see now why Dad had to leave our meeting so quickly this morning. And why it was so hard to get him to come back—even when one of his favorite horses was in labor. You are one of the pertiest things I've seen in a long time. Isn't she, son?" He pivoted slightly, letting go of her hand, and tapped the man behind him on the back.

Olivia hadn't even seen the stranger behind Mr. Redbourne unloading a cart stacked with boxes, but when he stood to his full height, he was hard to miss with his old, loose-fitting navy t-shirt and dark hair with eyes to match.

"It's a pleasure to meet you…son?"

He laughed loudly.

"The pleasure, ma'am, is all mine." The younger of the two men stepped forward and tipped his hat. "Wesley Redbourne, ma'am."

"Wesley."

"So, you're the one Grayson's been going on about all day. I can see why."

Were all of the Redbourne men so bold? And so handsome? Even the older men, were oozing sex appeal.

"Wes. Uncle Tad."

Olivia nearly jumped out of her skin at the sound of Holden's low, booming voice behind her.

When had he returned?

"I see you've both met our guest for the week at Silver Springs," he said as he threw a large brown shopping bag into the backseat of the truck.

"Grayson filled us in on *everything*." Wesley smiled at Holden in an oddly conspiratorial way as he loaded his box into the back of his own truck.

"Holden, do you have any idea who you've got here?" Tad asked his nephew, grabbing him by the shoulder and gesturing towards her. "Have you ever heard of Jack Irons, David Kellory, or Timothy Brandish?" he asked excitedly, naming off three of the most popular western writers ever. "She's right up there with them, I'm telling you…"

Olivia thought she might die. She loved to hear from her fans, sure, but this was verging on surreal. A real live cowboy was comparing her work to some of the greats. No pressure.

"This one knows how to weave a tale that'll get your heart pumping," he continued. "Adventure, mystery, and romance, of course," he added with a wink in her direction.

Heat flooded her cheeks and she didn't dare look up at Holden.

"Why, one night not too long ago, I didn't get to sleep until the wee hours of the morning. Wouldn't have been so bad, had the rooster waited a few more hours to tell me it was time for my chores."

"I remember that day. You fell asleep with your arms resting on the top of a shovel." Wesley laughed. He turned to her. "Sounds like you're quite talented, Miss Blake."

"You flatter me, Mr. Redbourne," she told Holden's uncle.

"Nah, just saying it how it is. If I remember correctly, she also has a degree in business from Stanford and a masters in psychology, was it, from the University of Colorado."

"Is that so?" Holden asked.

"It's so."

Olivia nodded. He must have read the last bio that her publicist had put out on the website.

"Smart, talented, beautiful—you're one special gal, Miss Blake."

"Well, I'm glad you enjoy my books, Mr. Redbourne." She needed to change the subject. "Do you all live around here?" she asked, suddenly wondering the odds of running into more of the Redbourne family.

Wesley finished loading the last of his boxes and stepped over next to Holden, slinging his arm around her host's shoulder.

"There are eleven of us. Seven of us still live at SilverHawk—in our own homesteads, of course. Hasn't my cousin here filled you in on how it all works?" He patted Holden's chest.

Eleven? If they all looked as good as these two, her retreats would sell out in minutes. Not that they'd been a part of the package. She looked at Holden, who adjusted the side of his glasses.

"She'll learn soon enough." He stepped away from Wesley, slipping out from beneath his arm, walked the few steps back to his truck, and opened the passenger side door. "Granddad will be expecting us."

Where had the time gone? Olivia looked at her watch. Five o'clock. It had been too long since she'd eaten supper any earlier than seven or even eight. And usually, that consisted of something she could either throw in the oven or the crockpot without a lot of preparation, or take out from Mr. Chu's.

"Yeah, we have to get going too. Come on, Dad," Wesley said, leaving the side door open as he ran around to the driver's seat. "Be safe on your way home, Holden," he said with a laugh and a wave.

Before Olivia joined Holden, she took Tad by the hand and leaned over to kiss him on the cheek. "It's been such a pleasure to meet you, Mr. Redbourne," she whispered with a smile and a light squeeze.

"We'll talk again soon," he called after her. "Rest assured."

She slipped into Holden's truck and he shut the door behind her.

The ranch was only a few miles away from town and Olivia had a lot of questions. One thing was for certain, this trip was going to be a lot more interesting than she'd originally expected.

CHAPTER FIVE

Holden wanted to strangle Wes, but for the life of him, he couldn't figure out why. He gripped the steering wheel tighter and twisted backward.

"Exactly how big is SilverHawk?"

The sound of Olivia's voice penetrated his ponderings and he glanced over at the woman who, in one day, had made him question his plans and what it was he wanted from the ranch. From his life. He didn't normally make decisions on a whim. He didn't question tradition—a person didn't throw away the hard work of others, he built on it and found ways to innovate better methods of doing things.

"Wesley said you all have your own homesteads. I'm guessing Silver Springs is yours, but what did he mean about 'how it all works?'"

Her question was simple enough, but not easy to answer. He thought for a few moments on how he could respond most effectively. And it hit him.

"SilverHawk is like one of your series' of books. It represents the series title, but each individual book, or ranch in this case, has a separate title." He dared a glance over at her.

She looked forward, out the windshield, nodding her head.

"Landon, Grayson, and I run Silver Springs and we work

mostly with beef cattle. Uncle Tad, Wes, and his brother Micah run Silver Canyon. They breed horses. Then, the rest of our cousins are split between Silver Oak and Silver Creek. They focus on the dairy and farming aspects of ranch life respectively."

"That finally makes sense." Her head bobbed up and down. "I didn't understand on the way up here why all of the ranches had 'silver' in the title, but you're all family."

"That's right. We—"

Thump. Thump. Thump. The low methodical sound was unmistakable.

"I think your tire is flat," Olivia told him as she strained against the window.

Of course it is.

Holden doubted it was a coincidence that they'd run into Wes in town and now they had a flat. Grayson must have filled their cousin in on the plan and he'd been more than happy to comply.

Number five on the list—get stranded.

He pulled the truck to a stop on the side of the road and hopped out to see the damage. It was flat all right. After a brief inspection, Holden determined that the valve cap had been tampered with and the air had been slowly leaking from the tire for what could have been hours. At least it didn't look like there was any permanent damage to either of the tires.

If he'd wanted to strangle Wes before, now the urge was ten-fold. The sun had dipped below the mountain and though there was still plenty of light, it was fading fast. He walked around to the side of the truck to the spare, but, to his chagrin, the spare had also been deflated.

With a silent plea for patience, he reached into his pocket for his cell, but it wasn't there. He'd left it sitting on the charger on the kitchen cabinet at home. He hung his head, wary of telling the city-slicker they'd have to walk the rest of the way.

"Looks like we're walking then," Olivia said from behind

him.

He whipped around, surprised to see her standing there also examining the tires.

"At least it's a beautiful night," she said, shrugging her shoulders. "Besides, if we were in the nineteenth century, we wouldn't have had a vehicle to ride in anyway. Right?" She sounded almost cheery. That surprised him.

"Yeah, but horses didn't generally get a flat either."

She looked up at him. "They…could…throw a shoe."

They both laughed. He liked that she could find something positive in the situation.

"Come on," he said. "It'll be faster through here." He pointed to the pasture on their left. "I'll come back for the bags after supper."

He locked the doors, then grabbed her hand as they ran across the street. He liked the feel of her hand in his, so he didn't let go until they reached the border of the Redbourne property-line. Holden watched as Olivia climbed up and over the fence without hesitation.

He followed.

"You've done this before," he said with a hint of admiration.

"I didn't always live in the city. I grew up in a small town with plenty of fences to climb. It wasn't on a ranch or anything, but our neighbors had horses. And a cow. They even let me milk her once."

"So, you've milked a cow too. Aren't you just full of surprises?"

She giggled.

"Have you always wanted to be a rancher?"

He'd asked himself that same question many times throughout the years.

"Truth is, I've tried other things. I worked for a large architecture firm while I was going to school. I experimented in an engineering lab. I even taught a few adjunct classes at the local university, but each time my heart led me back to the ranch. I love it here."

"I can see why," she said. "It's so peaceful, and I don't think you could paint a sunset more breathtaking than that." She pointed to the western sky.

"Of course, not, but I'd bet Landon could come close. He's the artist in the family. Many of his photos have been displayed in magazines and galleries across the country."

"Landon is a photographer?"

"Yes. You've seen some of his work displayed at the house."

"The photo of you looking out on the countryside."

"Yes. He calls that picture, 'Contemplation.'"

"He's very talented. Of course, it helps to have a good subject," she said, her smile reaching her lovely grey eyes.

Holden stopped for a moment and just watched as Olivia continued to look at everything with child-like awe. He'd opened up to her and that was not something he did easily. What was it about her that made him want to impress her? To trust her? To—

"Oh, fiddlesticks," she blurted as she froze in her tracks and looked down.

"What's wrong?" he asked as he caught up to her, laughing. No one used the word 'fiddlesticks' anymore, but it seemed fitting for an author of historical fiction.

"I think I just stepped in…in cow poo." She raised her hands up into the air and dropped them again. "It smells awful," her nose scrunched, "and it's all over my brand new boots."

Holden laughed again. "Well, I guess that's one way to break them in. At least we got them waterproofed first."

"True." Olivia resigned a laugh too. "But, can I just say, ewwww?"

"Wipe them off in the grass. They'll be fine."

"Easy for you to say, you're not covered in Eau-de-Pew!" She bent down to remove the boot and he took a step forward to help steady her.

Squish.

"Ack." Holden shook his head as his foot slid across another pile of dung. This was not his first rodeo. How had he missed that? Oh, yeah, he hadn't. The last thing he needed to do was slip and fall on his backside in front of the lady.

"HA!" Olivia burst out into laughter. "Don't worry," she said with a giggle lacing her voice, "just wipe them off in the grass. They'll be fine."

"Come on," he said in defeat as he dragged his foot over the grasses one way and then the other, attempting to rid his own boots of the clumped stench. "The homestead isn't much farther. If we hurry, we can make it there before it gets too dark to see where we're going."

When they finally reached the front steps, Holden looked down at his watch. If they hustled inside, there might still be food left on the table. He stopped short of the metal scraper embedded in the cement block at the base of the stairs. He lifted his foot and demonstrated how to best rid boots of the lingering manure stuck to the bottom. When he was done, he removed them and reached up for the hose hanging on its iron perch against the base of the house.

Olivia followed suit.

"That's a nifty little tool," she said with a smile as she pulled off her boots and waited while he washed the bottoms of his own. When they were clean, he gripped the kink in the line, but it slipped from his hand and sprayed Olivia in the face.

She gasped.

"Oh, I am so sorry," he said, but couldn't help the chuckle that threatened.

"I think you did that on purpose," she accused with a mock gasp as she wiped the excess water from her face. She opened one eye and looked at him, reaching for the hose.

"I don't think so," he said, taking a step away from her. "Why don't you just hand me your boots and I'll take care of them."

As she held out her boots to him, she reached for the hose and pulled it enough that it shot a stream of water directly into his own face. If it hadn't been so cold outside, he would have declared war, but as she slipped up the stairs in her socks, he thought better of it.

"I have brothers," she said with a grin. "Three of them. I learned a thing or two."

He laughed, sprayed off the boots, and joined her on the porch. He set the footwear next to the door. When he stood up, he became suddenly all too aware of how close they stood to each other. He could smell the sweet fragrance of her hair and he longed to reach out and touch the smoothness of her skin. He unwittingly leaned a little closer.

"If you don't mind," she said with an uneasy smile, "I think I'm just going to freshen up a bit and will join you shortly." She tucked a strand of wet hair behind her ear and bit her lip.

How did this woman have such an effect on him? It wasn't like he hadn't dated beautiful women before. He froze. He was not dating Olivia Blake.

"Thank you," she said, lightly tapping his chest with her fingertips, "for everything you did for me today."

Holden nodded, still a little taken back by the direction his thoughts had taken, and opened the door for her. She quickly ducked inside.

As he watched her jaunt down the hallway and disappear up the staircase, he realized that whether or not he'd wanted it, things *had* changed and for the first time in a long time, he didn't have a plan. He shook his dripping head. After stopping at the linen closet and toweling his hair dry, he headed into the dining room.

"I was just about to call in the cavalry." Granddad looked past him. "Where's Miss Blake? Isn't she with you?"

"Truck got a flat."

Grayson snorted.

"And you didn't have a spare?" Granddad asked, incredulity lining his voice.

"It's flat too."

His youngest brother stared intently at the cheesy potato casserole on his plate, a smirk twitching at his lips.

"What's going on with you today, son? It's not at all like you to be unprepared."

"It's nothing, Granddad. Gray will drive me out there after supper with the air compressor and we'll get it fixed up."

His grandfather glanced over at Grayson, then back at him. "And Miss Blake?"

"She'll be right down."

Landon walked into the dining room with a fresh full plate of food.

"I just heard about the truck, Hold," he said with a snicker.

Granddad raised a brow. "I don't know what's going on here, but see to it that Olivia feels at home."

"Yes, sir."

"And, that goes for the both of you too."

"Yes, sir."

CHAPTER SIX

Olivia snuck up the stairs and into her room. Once her door shut, she leaned up against it, unable to help the smile that seemed permanently embedded on her face. She pushed away and strolled into the bathroom where she glanced into the mirror and pinched her already flushed cheeks. She knew she should be telling herself to run, to get as far away from Holden Kane as possible, but there was something about him that made her feel like herself again. And it had been way too long.

Fate had been on her side when Ian Redbourne had stopped by her table at the Western Readers Convention book signing last month. They'd gotten to talking and he'd offered her a partnership that included the opportunity to host a retreat for her readers at one of his ranches in northern Colorado. How was she supposed to have known that the Redbournes owned the entire town of Silver Falls and all of its surrounding territories? She hadn't known what to expect, but was pleasantly surprised to find that they were a lot like the Blackwood family in her novels. Wealthy and attractive, but still down to earth and approachable.

She figured she shouldn't leave the others waiting any longer than necessary, so since they'd left all of her new clothing back in the truck, she slipped back into her maxi-skirt and peasant blouse, pulled the tie from her hair, and quickly brushed through her wet locks. She smiled again as she thought of the look on Holden's face when the sprayer hit him full force.

After she'd added a few twists and curls to her hair, and fastened them in place with several bobby pins, she reapplied a quick coat of mascara and chapstick. When she felt properly presentable, she headed back down the stairs and into the dining room where four very handsome men sat waiting to greet her.

They all pushed back from the table and stood up when they saw her.

"Livvy, I'm so pleased you have agreed to join us," Ian said as he moved to take her by the hand and lead her to an empty seat at the table. "I understand you have had quite the day."

She dared a glance at Holden, who locked her gaze with his own.

"It has certainly been an adventure."

"I'm guessing those are coming in spades around here."

A few snickers turned into chuckles, and then they all started laughing.

The rest of dinner was full of charming conversation and tales of humorous happenings and horror stories that had taken place on or around the ranch. Olivia wasn't sure whether they were trying to entice her to stay or push her away. She could see a lot of possibilities for her retreat and was looking forward to gaining more hands on experience at ranch life, but it had been a long day and she was tuckered out.

She brought her hand up to her mouth to cover the wide yawn that could not be stifled.

"We've kept you up way too late and we have an early start in the morning," Ian said with a curt nod, both of his hands palms down against the flat surface of the table.

They all pushed their chairs back as if on cue.

"Goodnight, Miss Blake," Holden said, tapping on the brim of his imaginary hat.

The sleeping butterflies reawakened in her belly when he

winked at her. From what she had gathered from their conversation at the dinner table, Holden was a very smart, objective man who generally gave little consideration to seemingly insignificant pleasantries. That may have sounded like the man she'd first met this morning, but now, she wasn't convinced. She'd seen how generous he could be. Protective.

"Goodnight, Mr. Kane," she returned the sentiment with a slight dip of her head and a smile she hoped touched her eyes.

"'Night, Olivia," Grayson said as he passed by her with his dirty dishes in hand. He was, by far, the most outgoing of the brothers. He smiled and winked. "I'm sure this will prove to be a very interesting week."

"I'm sorry you got stuck with the likes of this one all day, Olivia," Landon said as he set the last of the plates into the dishwasher and pushed start to begin the load. "I'd be happy to show you around a little tomorrow." Landon jabbed his older brother in the ribs and raised a brow—she guessed to gauge Holden's reaction to the offer.

Holden had a poker face if she ever saw one. Nothing. Not a smile. Not a grimace. Not a twitch. Nothing.

"Go to bed. We're starting early," he called after them as both Grayson and Landon headed down the hallway, presumably to their own bedrooms.

"Goodnight," Holden said again, pausing a moment when he met her eyes, then brushing past her on his way out.

"Rascals. The lot of 'em," Ian said with a laugh. "First day is always a bit of adjustment, but I'm confident this is the right place for you. And your fans," he added with a smile. "I'll be back in the morning and we can discuss the details." He winked. "Sleep tight."

"Thank you, Ian. I'll gather my thoughts and jot down a few notes before we meet tomorrow. I'm looking forward to the possibilities." Luckily, she had packed a notebook and several pens in her laptop case and wouldn't have to go begging for something to write on.

She clicked on the lamp on the nightstand next to her bed and realized that she had nothing to sleep in. At least she had remembered to pack a toothbrush, deodorant, and other necessary toiletries. As she stepped over to the window to close the curtains, she saw a shadow moving in the yard. She froze and jumped to the side of the glass panes, her heart thundering inside of her chest, her breaths barely squeaking in and out. She reached down very carefully and flipped off the lamp's switch, then dared another glance outside.

"He's not here. He's not here. He's not here," she chanted very quietly under her breath.

"Hurry up, Gray. I don't want to be gone all night." Holden's newly familiar voice, though distantly muffled, washed a sense of calm over her and she briefly closed her eyes with relief. Curious, she continued to watch as Grayson's shadowy figure loaded something bulky into the back of a truck. It clanked, metal against metal.

What are they doing?

Then she remembered that Holden had said he would go back for the bags after supper. She guessed the metal contraption was an air compressor to inflate the tires so he could drive his own truck back home.

Olivia had plenty to do with a deadline looming and a reader's retreat to plan. She would just wait up in the nice cozy overstuffed chair in the corner of the room and work until they returned.

As much as she hated to admit it, the idea of seeing Holden one more time before she drifted off to dreamland sounded very appealing. She grabbed a pencil, her laptop, and a notebook, and snuggled up with her legs tucked up beneath her into the long-seated chair.

What a day.

Her ears perked up at some sort of snorting sound. She looked up, listening more intently for the sound to repeat, and a slight movement caught her eye under the vanity. She leaned forward, squinting, but to no avail.

"Don't be so paranoid," she said aloud, chalking it up to nerves.

This is a safe place, she reminded herself. *He won't find you here.*

With one more glance at the dark space beneath the dressing table, she shook her head and returned her pencil to paper.

Now, what kind of trouble can these characters get into?

CHAPTER SEVEN

"Well," Grayson said in a conspiratorial manner as he climbed into the driver's seat of their granddad's truck, "I don't think she's found Darla yet."

"Gray!" Holden nearly shouted as he closed his eyes and placed his hand on the outside frame of the rolled down window. "You didn't."

His youngest brother stretched his mouth and chin in an 'oops' fashion and shrugged.

"I thought I told you we were going to nix the list."

"That was after I'd already released it in her room, and honestly, I'd forgotten about her until now."

They'd gotten the tires pumped up without much of a problem. Luckily, both the regular tire and the spare had been undamaged by the prank.

"Let's hope we find it before Granddad hears about it." Holden patted the door twice with a firm hand. "Follow me," he said as he quickly ran back to his own truck, jumped in, and started for home.

"Come on. Come on," he muttered under his breath, thumping the top of the steering wheel with his thumbs as he navigated the bumpy road back to the ranch.

When he pulled up into the front drive, he grabbed Olivia's

bags and hopped out, taking the porch steps two at a time. He threw open the front door, ran down the hallway, and up the stairs, but stopped short when he reached Olivia's room. Suddenly, her door burst open and she stepped into the hallway holding a long, fat bullsnake.

"Oh, Holden. I was just coming to find you." She met his eyes with a smile. "Look who I found crawling around in my room," she said as if it were the most natural thing in the world. She held the snake out to show him.

Holden shivered. He was not a fan of snakes—especially the kind that looked so much like rattlers. Their nephew had raised the bullsnake from a hatchling and it had grown accustomed to people, but harmless or not, Holden did not like it. Cows, horses, pigs—even chickens—were preferable to any animal in the reptile or amphibian families.

"Where's her cage?" she asked.

"How…?" He'd expected a frantic houseguest, a little bit of chaos, or at least a screaming damsel in distress, but she surprised him yet again. "How did you know she was a pet?" he asked, breathless from his grand gesture to save her.

"Bullsnakes are generally scared of people and this one, well, she slithered right up to me. I don't know that I've ever seen one do that before. You have her trained very well."

"Oh, she's not mine. She belongs to my nephew."

Grayson ran into the house and up the stairs, then stopped with a jolt, staring at Olivia, looking as dumbfounded as Holden felt.

"I'm…not sure what to say right now," Gray told them.

Olivia laughed.

"Don't look so surprised. I did a lot of research on bullsnakes for my first book. I even hired a snake wrangler." She laughed. "The things you learn in the name of research."

"A snake wrangler?" Gray's eyes grew wide. "I didn't even know such a thing existed."

"Her cage?" Olivia asked again.

"Oh, yeah. I'll be right back."

Sometimes it was hard to believe that his little brother was already twenty-one and a part-time deputy sheriff. He still seemed like a frat boy with his love of practical jokes and his fascination with childish things.

"Not much of a snake fan, huh?"

Holden raised a brow. "I have just never seen the need for them."

"Did you know that they eat mice, rats, and other small rodents? Not that I would ever want a snake as a pet, but I can see how they might earn their keep."

"A cat."

"I'm sorry?"

"A cat. We'd get a cat if Landon wasn't so allergic."

"I like cats. And dogs," she said. "I tend to prefer mammals as pets."

Finally, Grayson found his way back up the stairs with the cage and took the animal from Olivia.

"Darla, I really do hate your stinking guts."

They all laughed.

"Sorry she got loose in your room, Olivia," Grayson said, then turned to Holden. "I'll make sure she gets back over to Silver Oak first thing in the morning."

Holden nodded.

"Goodnight. Again. Olivia," Gray said before heading back down to his room.

"Goodnight, Grayson."

"I thought you might be needing these." He handed her all of the shopping bags they'd gotten in town today, except the last one Holden had purchased. He would save that one for later.

"Thank you." Olivia reached out to take them, her hand brushing lightly against his. "I wasn't sure what I was going to sleep in tonight." She looked up at him, her eyes wide, brilliant. "I mean, um...it'll be nice to have some new pajamas to sleep in."

She'd brushed her hair, which now hung down her shoulders, and she had cleaned her face of any make-up. He'd been around plenty of women who would never have allowed any man to see them without their social masks or perfect façades.

Olivia was different.

"I thought that might be the case." He managed a smile. "Goodnight, Miss Blake." He reached up to tip his hat, only to realize it wasn't there. Heat crept up his neck.

"Goodnight, Mr. Kane." She leaned against the doorframe, holding the bags up close to her.

He nodded and made his way back down the stairs.

Instead of heading straight into bed, Holden stopped in the library and looked over his grandfather's shelves. It didn't take long for him to find what he'd been looking for—*The Rancher's Winter Bride*, the first book in Olivia's Blackwood series. He looked over his shoulder to make sure no one had seen him take it, then shoved it under his arm and headed down toward his room.

It was time to see what all the fuss was about.

Chapter One.

CHAPTER EIGHT

The excitement of being on the ranch kept Olivia from sleeping as well as she would have liked. Nevertheless, it allowed her to mull over and devise a few plans in her mind for what she wanted to do for her reader's retreat. By five o'clock she was done trying to sleep any longer and decided her time would be better spent doing something productive. So, instead of waiting another hour for her alarm to go off, she simply got up, got dressed, and headed downstairs.

"You're up early."

Olivia nearly jumped out of her socks. She was surprised to see Holden sitting in the adjacent mud room pulling on his boots.

"You startled me," she said, her hand flat against her chest.

"Sorry. I guess it's one of the hazards of getting up before the rooster crows," he said as he stood up.

Her mouth went dry. Holden's shirt dangled open, revealing his very fit physique. She'd had a witty retort, but for the life of her, she could not think of what it was. She sucked in a breath as the tanned flesh of his chiseled navel slowly disappeared as his fingers worked to fasten each button.

Look up! she demanded—pleaded with herself.

After a moment, she was finally able to divert her gaze to

his face, though with his sexy blue eyes and dimpled smile, she was doomed. He was a *very* handsome man.

"I brought your boots in," he said, jutting his chin toward the fireplace. "They should be nice and toasty by now," he said as he took a step toward her and reached up, pulling something from the cupboard above her. "Would you like to help me collect the eggs?"

She cleared her throat and forced herself to focus on his words.

"Eggs? Yes. I would like that. Very much. Mmhmmm. Yep."

He laughed. "Are you all right?" he asked as he looked down at her, his brows etched together.

She didn't trust herself to speak again, so she folded her lips together and simply nodded.

"Well, what are you waiting for?"

She stood there a moment, unsure what he was insinuating. *The boots.*

She dodged her way around him, found a seat in the little wooden back chair near the fireplace, and tugged on her warmed boots. She glanced up to see Holden tucking his shirt into his waistband.

She exhaled smartly, then jumped up and met him at the door.

Holden handed her a basket and the new jacket they had picked up for her in town.

"Ready?"

As they approached the pen, he took a few minutes to explain what she needed to do. They had over twenty chickens in the enormous coop and she'd never actually been in one, so she wasn't sure what to expect.

"Remember, even though the chickens can't bite, they can peck. And it'll hurt. So, do your best not to get pecked." He opened the pen door and walked with her to the coop gate.

"Gee, thanks for that," she said as she cautiously

approached the door.

"After we collect all the eggs, we need to let them out into the pen to roam around."

"Why does that sound like one of those things that is easier said than done?" she asked as she approached the miniature-sized barn-style building.

"Don't worry. You'll do just fine."

Once they got inside, Olivia took a moment to study it. If she ever used collecting eggs in one of her books, she wanted to make sure it would be as close to real-life as possible. Several cubicle-style boxes sat against the wall along with a few heavy baskets lined with straw bedding—most of them occupied by sleeping hens. One chicken had perched itself on one of the shelves, and a couple of them roamed around the elevated wooden floor.

"It'll go much easier if you don't wake them," he told her, lifting one hen very carefully and retrieving her egg.

It didn't look too difficult.

Olivia followed his example to the tee and when she'd successfully collected her first egg, she nearly dropped it before she could get it into the basket.

"Careful," he reminded her in low, quiet tones.

COCK-A-DOODLE-DOO!

In moments, the coop was a muddle of chaos as the chickens awoke all at once at the rooster's crow. Amidst the commotion, several of the hens left their roosts with the eggs still lying neatly in the straw—making for easy collection.

"Do we have them all?" she asked loudly, counting the eggs in her basket.

Holden held up a finger. "I'll get the last one and meet you out in the pen."

Olivia opened the coop door and stepped out onto the ramp, but was greeted by a strutting rooster, eying her from the bottom of the plank.

"Holden?" she called nervously over her shoulder in a quiet

voice.

The animal was more than twice the size of any of the hens inside.

"Holden," she called again. "There's a rooster out here that doesn't look very happy with me." She could hear the slight shake in her voice and chastised herself for her cowardice.

You can do this. You are smart. You are brave. You've got this.

When she took another slow step down the run, the rooster crowed loudly and started to chase her up the ramp. She stumbled backward over the top rung, but managed to knock Holden back far enough that they could close the door. She stood with her rear-end against the wood, set the basket down—grateful the eggs had not been broken in the process—and placed her hands on her knees, her heart pumping heavily inside her chest.

"We're trapped," she said breathily, then started to laugh.

"I see you've met Brewster."

"You have a rooster named Brewster?"

"Sad, isn't it? He's the meanest, orneriest rooster you'll ever meet, but you just have to show him who's boss."

"And how exactly am I supposed to do that?" She shook her head.

"So, you can hold a bullsnake without a second thought, but you're scared of a little old rooster."

"Little?" she asked incredulously. "Have you seen that thing?"

He was right though.

Buck up, Liv.

"All right. Since I don't want to be stuck in here all morning, tell me what I need to do."

"I'll show you what you'll need to do next time. Without gloves and a thicker coat, he'll eat you alive."

"That's encouraging."

Holden stepped in front of her and opened the door. Brewster was not there waiting for them. Maybe there wouldn't have to be anymore chicken related lessons today after all. Olivia picked up the basket of eggs and looped it over her forearm, then placed her hand against Holden's strong back and followed him down the ramp. They left the coop door open so the hens could come down into the pen at their leisure.

Olivia looked from one side to the other—still no Brewster in sight. Her feet hit the dirt.

COCK-A-DOODLE-DOO!

"Run!" Holden yelled, pointing toward the pen gate.

Then she saw him, the rooster, running toward them faster than she'd ever seen a chicken move. With one hand trying to hold the eggs as still as possible, she ran.

Peck.

Ouch. He'd gotten her on the back of the leg. Luckily she was wearing jeans and not her black yoga pants. That could have been really bad. She didn't look back. She just continued toward the gate as fast as she thought she could go with her delicate cargo.

Landon appeared on the other side of the gate and swung it open as she approached. Once she was clearly through, he closed it again, trapping the rooster in the pen with Holden and the hens.

"Are you all right, ma'am?" Landon said, the rays of light from the morning sun adding just the right backlight to his masculine cowboy appearance.

"Thank you. That was perfect timing."

She turned around to see Holden chasing after the rooster with his hands extended out in front of him. It didn't take long before he caught the thing around the middle, scratching, twisting, and pecking. He tucked it up under his arm and calmly walked around the pen. He caught her stare and with a smile walked toward her, opened the gate, and walked through—the rooster still in his grasp.

"See," he said. "That wasn't so hard."

"You wanted me to…catch the rooster?" she asked in

disbelief.

Peck.

"Dam…" he glanced over at her, "…-rn—darn it all," he corrected.

Brewster had drawn blood from Holden's hand.

"How did Brew get in the chicken's pen?" Landon asked his brother. "I thought we weren't—"

DING. CLANG. DING. CLANG. DING.

Everyone looked toward the house where a plump woman in a blue dress and an apron stood ringing an old-fashioned triangle.

"So, I forgot to tell you. Granddad hired Mrs. Davenport to come and cook for the week," Landon said. By the look on his face, he may as well have been licking his lips. "I guess he wanted to make sure that Olivia had a good culinary experience as well."

Holden looked down at her.

"Hungry?"

"Yes, sir."

He took the rooster back to his separate pen. Olivia was amazed that when he turned it loose, it simply started pecking at the ground and strutting around as if nothing had happened.

When Holden returned, he also acted like it had been no big deal, but she could see the smile dancing around in his eyes.

"Allow me," he said, reaching out to take the basket from her.

She relinquished the eggs and turned to walk up the back porch steps. When she got to the top, he rushed to get the door and she noticed the blood that had made a trail between his forefinger and thumb.

"That's a lot of blood. We should get it cleaned up," she said—not that her first aid training would do her any more good after sitting on a shelf for three years, than simply knowing how to clean it with some peroxide, then dress it with anti-biotic ointment and a bandage. "Chickens can carry all sorts of bacteria and diseases."

"It's nothing," he said just like she expected he would.

"I insist," she replied with a raised brow.

He chuckled and pushed open the door.

The savory scent of fresh cooked bacon wafted through the air and Olivia's mouth watered. This Mrs. Davenport worked fast. It had been a long time since she'd had a home-cooked breakfast. Cold cereal and a piece of fruit or juice had become her recent go-to morning meal with her busy schedule and she had missed the finer points of breakfast like pancakes, eggs, and bacon.

Holden set the eggs down on the kitchen cabinet and motioned for her to follow him.

The main floor bathroom was beautiful with rich grooved wood linoleum and a tiled shower. He opened the cabinet behind the door and pulled out a box full of medical supplies.

Olivia turned on the water in the sink and washed her hands thoroughly. She left it running when she was done. Once it was warm, she moved away from the sink to allow room for Holden.

"Wash them really good," she said with authority.

"Yes, ma'am."

When he finished, the wound was still bleeding pretty steadily.

If chickens were anything like cats, she knew the more it bled the better it would be to help clean out the toxins and possible debris. Couldn't hurt. She grabbed one of the small clean towels from the box for him to dry his hand.

"I'm guessing collecting eggs will not be on your retreat agenda," he said with a smile as she patted the area dry.

"On the contrary, as long as that devil of a bird stays in his own pen, collecting eggs was quite the experience." With a large cotton swab she'd soaked in peroxide, she brushed over the puncture in order to see the wound more clearly.

He didn't move, but the muscles in his jaw flexed.

Olivia held his hand out over the sink and poured directly

from the bottle. It fizzed a little at first, but after a moment it ran clean. She used another cotton swab to scrub the affected area, rinsed it, then dried it off before applying the ointment. Blood still trickled from the wound, so she quickly wrapped it with a large adhesive bandage.

Her fingers lingered a little longer than necessary. She liked the warmth of his hand in hers and she looked up at him.

"All done," she said with a sense of satisfaction. "Now, that wasn't so hard, was it?" she mimicked his earlier comment.

"I couldn't have done it better myself," he said as he put everything back in the medical box and returned it to the cupboard. "Now, can we eat?"

"Yes. I'm starving and it smells so good."

Her stomach grumbled.

They both laughed.

CHAPTER NINE

The rest of the day proved fairly uneventful. Granddad had decided to take Olivia for a tour of the other ranches at SilverHawk after breakfast. They'd been gone all day and it irritated Holden that he hadn't been able to stop thinking about the woman the entire time.

He sat out on the porch in one of the old rocking chairs that had been passed down through generations and watched as the sun slowly began its descent on the mountainside. He'd finished up his chores early and had taken the time to sneak in a few chapters of Olivia's book. He had to give her credit. It was pretty good—for a romance novel.

Tomorrow would be a full day. It was time to check the herds and make sure that the mamas were still feeding their babies. Calving season this year had been pretty busy and had lasted longer than most, but all the new additions had been tagged, given their shots, and the males banded—except for the two purebreds that would be raised as bulls.

He wasn't sure how Olivia would react to the long ride, but he had a feeling she'd overcome this obstacle with her usual vibrant optimism.

Grayson pulled up into the drive and climbed out of the truck. Holden hadn't seen his brother all day as he'd taken a shift at the sheriff's office and then had gone over to Silver Canyon to help Wes and Micah with some of the new horses that had come in.

Holden tucked his book into his jacket.

"Where is everyone?" Gray asked as he approached the porch.

"Granddad decided to give Olivia a tour of SilverHawk. Landon is in his studio. And the new hands are having a meeting out in the bunkhouse with Joe."

Grayson sat down next to Holden and released a drawn-out sigh.

"Long day?"

"You could say that."

"Some idiot climbed the fence in Old Lady Haskell's yard and cut a good dozen roses from her prize bushes. Gave her quite the scare. Now, who would do that?"

"I guess that's a more interesting case than having to find little Shirley Mavis's baby doll."

"You mock, but we found that doll hanging from the trellis just below Johnny Willis's bedroom window. Now, there's a miscreant child if I ever met one."

Holden laughed.

"Speaking of mysteries. I'd like to know how Brewster got out into the chicken pen this morning. I thought I'd made myself clear about that list."

"It wasn't me, Hold. I swear. What happened? Did Olivia get hurt?"

Holden rubbed the section of his flesh that had been punctured by the rooster. "No, but I think that devil of a bird needs some breeding hens."

They both laughed.

"Oh, by the way, Wes said he didn't have anything to do with the air being let out of your tires last night. He said he didn't even realize you were in town until he saw you with Olivia."

There *had* been another car parked between their trucks, but if Wes hadn't done it...

It just didn't make any sense. It was too much of a coincidence. The hairs on the back of his neck stood on end.

It wasn't like him to worry—especially about someone he'd just met, but Olivia and his grandfather had been gone a long time. Almost too long. SilverHawk was big and there was a lot to see for someone looking to do business here, but he couldn't shake the bad feeling that washed over him.

His phone rang as if on cue, and he let out an uneasy breath.

"It's Granddad," he said as he picked it up.

Everything was fine.

Their cousin's wife had made them dinner and then they'd stopped off at the Community Center in town to introduce Olivia to the local book club members. He could just imagine the reaction of those ladies at meeting a famous author. He had to stop himself from rolling his eyes. He was beginning to see that there was more to her than the fluff he'd believed her books to be. He'd been wrong about her. And her books. And that didn't happen very often.

A phone call would have been nice. He hadn't been able to say the words aloud or he might have given his granddad, or Grayson for that matter, the wrong idea.

"I think I'm going to call it a night," Holden said as he stood up out of the chair. Olivia's book tumbled out onto the porch. He'd completely forgotten he'd tucked it in his jacket.

Grayson reached down to pick it up. "What are you reading?"

Holden wanted to wipe the widespread grin right off of Grayson's face as he handed it over.

"You've got a thing for the pretty romance novelist, don't you, Hold?"

"Get some sleep," he said, snatching the book from his brother's hand. "We've got a big day ahead of us tomorrow."

Grayson laughed. "Now it all makes sense."

"Shut up. Love you. Goodnight," he said, walking into the

house, allowing the door to snap shut behind him.

Though distant with a wall between them, Holden could still hear the chuckle in Gray's voice as he called back. "Goodnight."

CHAPTER TEN

Eight hours in and out of a saddle and Olivia was ready to head back to the homestead and crawl into a nice hot, soothing bath. They'd been riding all day out to the many pastures of SilverHawk to check on the hundreds of new calves that had been born already this year, and then herding them into fields flourishing with growth.

Two beautiful border collies had been trained to guide the herd and she was amazed at how efficiently they handled the cattle.

"Over here," Landon called out from his position by the stream.

"Let's go see what he's found," Holden said.

Several of the men gathered around where Landon waited, standing next to his horse.

"Looks like this one's brand new," Landon said. "She's hardly been licked and I can't seem to find which one could be her mama. She hasn't been tagged."

Holden glanced around. "It's not often that a mama will abandon her new baby, but if she was a heifer—a first time mother—she may not have known what to do with the baby and wandered away."

Olivia appreciated the insight. Most of her research had

taken her to horse ranches and she knew very little about cattle.

"It's getting pretty dark out here. We'll have to come out at first light and see if we can't find her mama."

"Wait. You're just going to leave her here? Alone? Without anyone to take care of her?" Olivia couldn't believe what she was hearing.

"She'll be fine through the night," Holden said in a voice she was sure was meant to reassure her. He herded the baby toward the straw lined structure in the middle of the field.

Olivia clicked her heels against the mare she rode and followed behind Holden.

"She's in a good place and getting the mama to come back and claim the calf is in the best interest of everyone," he told her as the calf stepped with wobbly legs to the open section of the shelter.

"That's not going to happen," the foreman, Joe, said as he joined the group. "I found her lying down just over the ridge. Prolapsed uterus. It doesn't look like she's been dead long, so it is possible that she already fed the calf."

Holden dropped his head. That was not the news he'd been hoping for.

"There is no way to tell for sure. So, we don't have much time to get some colostrum into her system."

Joe nodded. "And Miss Blake might be right about it being too dangerous to leave the little one out here alone."

A distant howl caught Olivia's attention.

"Is that wolves?" she asked, fearing even more for the newborn calf.

"Coyotes," Joe replied. "Saw a few of them hiding in the brush. I doubt they'll leave the calf alone."

Olivia sat up a little taller in her saddle. "Can we take her back with us?"

Everyone seemed to be waiting for Holden's command.

After a few moments, he dismounted.

"Landon, take Olivia and Grayson and go get the truck and

a bottle with a packet of frozen colostrum. Joe, tell the others to head back. We're done for the day."

"Yes, sir."

"I'll wait here with the calf." Holden pulled a rifle from the holster on the side of his horse and nodded at his brothers.

"I'm staying." Olivia swung her leg around and slid down off the mare. Her legs wobbled and she was afraid she might make a fool of herself by face-planting into the snow-encrusted dirt, so she held onto the side of the saddle until she was confident she could walk without falling. She had a new empathy for the little one who'd just been given a chance at life.

Holden captured and held her gaze for some time before he glanced up at his brother and nodded. The men immediately turned their horses around and headed for home.

Olivia admired the respect between siblings. It was obvious that Landon and Grayson both looked up to their older brother.

"You are something else, Olivia Blake," he said as he collected the reins for both horses in his hands and made his way to the cozy little outbuilding.

She smiled.

Though a roof covered the majority of the structure, and wooden slats several inches apart served as walls, the place was still exposed to the evening air. There were dozens of stones of varying sizes lining the base of the semi-enclosed space and she wondered what they might be used for.

"Wait here," Holden told her, handing her his gun and the horses' reins. He opened the gate and went inside.

Olivia glanced over the top of the slatted wall as he pulled a bale of straw down off a short stack in the corner, and quickly spread it across the floor in two of the three stalls. He grabbed another one and repeated the process in the more spacious, but still enclosed side of the building. When he was finished, he shook out the blankets that had been covering the straw and draped them over the wall. He stepped back outside and took the horses from her, leading them into the stalls.

"We need to collect that calf," he said as he opened a small cupboard built into the center of the building. He pulled out a few well-worn towels and a stack of something that looked like badly folded blankets and set them on the dry ground next to her, then motioned for her to join him. "I'm going to need you to man the gate. I'll go round her up and as soon as she comes inside, I'll need you to close it and lock it like this." He demonstrated how to work the latch on the gate.

She nodded. "Got it."

He took the gun from her and set it down at the edge of the stall, then swung the gate wide, heading out into the growing darkness toward the feeble newborn. After he'd gotten behind the little thing, he started making some of the noises Olivia had listened to all throughout the day.

"Yip! Yip! Hi-ya!" He ran from side to side like she'd seen the herding collies do earlier in the day, directing the youngling where to go.

She had to laugh.

Once the calf ran past her, she swung the gate shut and locked it as Holden had shown her. She dusted off her hands, clapping them together with a laugh.

"You did it," she said, beaming up at him as he approached. He stopped mere inches from her, reaching up to take the blanket from the wall behind her.

"*We* did it," he corrected.

A light breeze blew across the meadow provoking goosebumps to trail down Olivia's arms. She shivered.

"We need to get a fire started. The last thing I need is for you to freeze to death out here," Holden said.

"I'll be fine." But the warmth of a fire sounded delightful.

He regarded her with a look that said he didn't believe her, then disappeared for a moment around the side of the building.

Olivia remembered the stones surrounding the structure. She collected a couple of them at a time and carried them to a place just to the side of the gate of the small open corral housing the calf and made a circle with the stones touching each other.

When Holden returned, he had a blanket-full of chopped wood cradled in his arms.

"Look at you," he said with a nod. "You must have been a Girl Scout."

"No sir, I just have a dad who enjoys camping. Every summer since I was old enough to walk, we've gone up into the mountains for a family vacation."

"Three brothers and a dad who took you camping. No wonder you seem to fit right in around here." He dumped the wood out of the blanket, shook it out, and folded it in half, setting it down on the ground behind her. "Sit."

She wasn't about to argue, unsure of how much longer her legs were going to support her.

Holden reached under the gate and grabbed a large handful of straw. He placed it in the center of the ring and took a few minutes to carefully build the familiar teepee over the top of the dry kindling, using the smaller pieces first and the bigger ones on top.

"Don't tell me you are going to rub two sticks together to start the fire," she said, only half kidding.

He snorted a breathy laugh, shaking his head, and stood up straight. He walked into the stalls and came out with a small cinch bag and his rifle. He pulled out a box of light anywhere matches and held them up.

"Boy Scout?"

"Yes, ma'am," he replied with pride as he knelt down. "Eagle." He struck the match and held it in the open space between two larger logs, until the straw caught fire. Then he leaned down and blew softly. "I'm always prepared." He looked at her. "Well...almost always."

It didn't take long for the flames to rise. The warmth felt wonderful on her hands and face. Holden sat down next to her, his back resting up against the building's gate, his legs stretched out in front of him.

"So, I never heard how your meeting went with Granddad yesterday."

Olivia wrapped her arms around her bent knees. "It was good. Ian is a good man." She dropped her head and stared into the fire. "Honestly, I thought I would be coming here to finalize a business proposal that would help to further my career. My publisher is always trying to think of new ways to market me and my books, and we thought this would be a great adventure that would provide a real experience for my fans. Nineteenth century living at its finest."

"And now?"

She glanced over at him, his eyes fixed intently on her. "Now…" she glanced up at the first twinkling star to appear. "Now, I think your granddad was a Godsend. This place. You."

Another breeze sent a chill down her back and she started to tremble, unsure whether or not it was only from the cold.

"Come here," Holden said quietly.

She looked over at him and he had an arm stretched out to her. She scooted back and snuggled into his warmth, enjoying the feel of him next to her and reveling in the fact that she fit perfectly beneath his arm. Like a couple of puzzle pieces.

He rubbed her shoulders and pulled her in tight against him, wrapping the edges of the blanket up and over their legs. She rested her head up against him and closed her eyes.

"They should be back anytime now," Holden said, squeezing her closer.

"What do *you* think about this whole reader's retreat idea?"

He didn't respond.

She raised her head enough that she could see his face. His eyebrows had creased together and he stared studiously into the night sky.

She returned her head to his shoulder, content to sit there in silence.

"I had a different plan for the ranch," he finally said. "I thought I had everything figured out, but when I heard about you and your reasons for visiting Silver Springs, I must admit, I was more than a little apprehensive."

"And now?" she used his own question against him.

He chuckled.

"Now," he paused and she wondered if he were just doing it for the effect. "I think that I would make a wonderful Bentley Blackwood."

She pushed herself up and looked at him again. "Have you...read my books?"

"Just the one," Holden said with a laugh. "I'm not done yet, but..."

"And?" She knew she was fishing, but she truly wanted to know what he thought.

"I think you are one very talented woman."

She bit her lip.

"Really?"

"Really," he said, a soft smile touching his face.

He leaned down, his lips so close to hers she could almost taste them.

Light beams from the truck bounced over their position on the ground. The sound of dirt and gravel beneath the wheels unmistakable.

"They have perfect timing," Holden groaned as he pushed himself up off the ground, then held a hand out to help her to a standing position.

Olivia's backside and legs groaned in protest. At least she'd gotten more sleep last night than the night before. But she had a feeling she would sleep better tonight than she had in a long time.

Grayson was the first to hop out of the truck. She could have sworn there was a look passed between the two brothers.

It didn't take long to get the calf loaded into the back of the truck. Holden put out the fire, then retrieved the horses from the outbuilding, but just the thought of crawling into the saddle made Olivia's backside hurt even more.

"Gray, you can ride in the back with the calf," Holden said. "Landon, Joe, you two take the horses. Stay close behind us. We'll take it slow. Miss Blake, you'll be with me in the truck."

Relief washed over her and she exhaled loudly.

They all laughed as if in understanding.

A comfortable silence rested between her and Holden as they drove back to Silver Springs. The day had taken its toll and, more than once, Olivia found herself drifting off to sleep."

"We're here," Holden said, reaching over and touching her lightly on the arm.

Olivia opened her eyes.

"That was fast."

Holden chuckled. "Funny how sleeping is almost as good as time travel."

"What time is it?"

"Nearly ten."

Olivia sat up and turned to see Grayson and the others unloading the calf from the back of the truck.

"Is she all right?" she asked as she clicked open the seatbelt and opened the door.

"She'll be just fine, thanks to you. Gray already fed her on the way back and now they'll take her into the barn where Granddad has a little area made up for her to sleep.

Olivia waddled around the truck and watched as the little calf disappeared inside the barn. Every muscle in her body cried out for relief.

"I don't suppose you all have a massage therapist on call," she said as she joined Holden leaning against the bed of his truck.

"I'm afraid not."

"I'll have to consider hiring one to come in whenever we have a retreat. Us city-slicking folks might not make it otherwise." She rubbed her backside. "A hot bath and a massage, add in some of that home cooking and you might not ever get me to leave."

"Promise?"

Silence.

"You hold up your end of the bargain and I'll hold up mine."

"I guess I should whip you up something for dinner, then."

"A man who cooks. I like it."

Holden smiled, but didn't say anything more.

"It was a good thing you did tonight. You're a good man too, Holden Kane." She pushed against him and away from the truck. "Goodnight," she said with a wave, but he caught her by the wrist and pulled her back against him, sliding his free hand along her jawline and behind her head as he guided her face toward him, capturing her lips with his own.

The warm sensations that had started at her core quickly spread through every inch of her entire body. His masterful kiss teased her, taunted her, and filled her with the kind of hope she'd only believed existed in fiction. It had only been a few days, but it was as if they'd always known each other, but had forgotten for a while. She knew it might seem silly, but she couldn't explain the connection she felt with him and being in his arms just felt...right.

He broke away, still only inches away from her. "Goodnight, Miss Olivia Blake," he said before climbing back into his truck and pulling forward into the drive.

Her fingers moved to her lips, still tingling from the sensation of his kiss. She stood there for a few more moments, then hastily climbed the porch steps and headed for her bedroom.

It had been a bone-tired kind of exhausting, pain-staking, heart-wrenching long day and Olivia wouldn't have changed a minute of it. As sore as her rear end and leg muscles were, they were a vivid reminder of all the possibilities ahead of her. Ahead of them.

Maybe she was reading more into that kiss than was there, but nothing with Jason had ever felt like this. Maybe Holden didn't feel the same, but for a romance novel kind of love, she was willing to take a chance.

When she reached her room, she slipped inside and shut the door, leaning against it, her eyes closed. She touched her lips again and exhaled firmly.

I've never been happier than I am right now.

With an excited, breathy giggle, she pushed away from the door and headed for the bathroom. Something strange and morbidly familiar caught her eye.

She froze.

No! No, no, no, no no!

Slowly, she pivoted around to see the object that had captured her attention and dropped to her knees on the floor.

Roses. One dozen black roses sat on her nightstand tied up neatly with long strands of red ribbon.

Her heart began to race.

It was getting harder to breathe.

NO!

How had he found her?

She dragged herself across the wooden floorboards until she reached the table. With a trembling hand, she pulled at the white corner of the crumpled paper sticking out from beneath the vase.

Slowly, she unfolded the message. It was a to-do list. Several thick, red checkmarks glared back at her from the page.

Disconnect electronics. Check.

Introduce the worst jobs on the ranch. Check.

Flatten tires—make her walk long distance. Check.

Release rooster in chicken pen. Check.

She quickly skimmed over the rest of the list until she came to the last item. In the same red ink as the checkmarks, but different handwriting than the rest and in all capital letters, were four words that made her blood run cold.

GET RID OF HIM.

An eerie chill fell over her body. She glanced up. Pinned to the wall was a photograph of her with Holden. A thick red circle drawn around his head, a heavy slash mark through his face.

Tears welled up in her eyes as she ripped the picture from the wall.

This can't be happening. Not again.

CHAPTER ELEVEN

"What has gotten into you, big brother?" Landon asked when Holden walked into the barn whistling.

He didn't respond, just picked up the towel at Grayson's feet and started drying off the newborn. Her fluffy brown fur contrasted greatly with the white of her face.

"Holden's gotten himself a girlfriend," Grayson teased as he piled the blankets they'd used to keep the baby cow warm on the ride home into a basket to be washed.

"You mean, Olivia?" Landon asked with interest.

"Didn't you see the way they were all snuggled up out at the shelter?" Grayson raised his eyebrows multiple times. "He likes her."

"Is that true?" Landon asked as he poured some iodine into a small cup.

Without the assistance of her mama and the nutrients from her milk, the calf would be more prone to illness and infection. They needed to do everything in their control keep her healthy.

Landon and Grayson both stared at him. Waiting.

"Miss Blake is smart and talented—"

"And beautiful," Landon filled in.

"And successful," Grayson added.

"Yes," Holden said, "she is all of those things…"

"So, that's a yes? You do like her," Landon affirmed as Gray laid the calf down on her side, allowing him to dip her naval in the red disinfectant without having it get everywhere.

"Okay," Holden relented. "I like her." He didn't know why it was so hard to admit. He hadn't felt this light in a long time. "What if I told you that I think I...love...her?"

"What?" both brothers exclaimed at once.

"You, my dear brother who would never even admit to kissing a girl, are telling us you are in love?" Landon nodded appreciatively. "She has gotten under your skin."

"It's only because she met him before she met me," Grayson teased. "Seriously, Hold, I've seen the way you look at each other and I say if it's right, it's right."

"I agree. Go for it."

He would have never guessed that it would take a spunky romance novelist to breathe life into his overly organized world. Beautiful and smart, witty and caring, he couldn't wait to spend more time getting to know her.

"You do realize you are going to need to romance this girl, right?"

"How?" Holden asked, afraid he wouldn't be able to live up to Olivia's standards.

"You know that book you've been reading?" Gray asked as he leaned back against the wall on his stool. "She wrote it, man. You will never have a better guide book to her heart than that."

"Wait. You've been reading her books?" Landon asked incredulously. "Which ones?"

"The Rancher's Winter Bride," Holden responded, taken back a little by the question.

"I loved that one," Landon admitted.

Holden looked at his brother, shock not quite covering what he was feeling.

"I like her books," Landon shrugged. "Get over it."

"The two of you are as crazy as Granddad. Romance books are for girls...women. Not men," Grayson chimed in.

"Just because you hide the books behind your *Smalltown Justice* magazines, doesn't mean we don't know what you're really reading, Gray," Landon teased.

Grayson returned the front two legs of his stool back to the floor with raised brow and a haughty smile, turning his attention back to his oldest brother. "You can do this, Hold."

"Just tell us what you need us to do."

"Can I get back to you on that?"

"Of course," Landon nodded curtly. "Just don't wait too long. Olivia is a one-in-a-lifetime kind of girl."

"I know."

"Well, that settles that. I think we're all done here," Grayson said, stripping off his blue latex gloves and tossing them in the trash. "I'm beat."

The calf laid down in the grass. She'd had quite a long day too.

"Are you on shift tomorrow?" Holden asked Gray as they turned off the lights and all walked out of the barn together.

"Yes. I should be grateful the worst thing we see around here are stolen roses. But sometimes, I wish there would be something actually interesting to investigate."

Landon snorted. "I heard the book club is trying to decide if they are going to make a calendar of the most eligible bachelors in Silver Falls. A sheriff and a rancher, I think you'd be at the top of the list."

"Go to bed, you two." Holden pushed his brothers toward the house. Although he enjoyed the friendly banter, it was late.

"Night, Hold," Landon said, patting him on the shoulder. "Congrats on the girl."

Holden couldn't stifle the grin that spread across his face.

"See ya in the morning," Grayson said with a dip of his head.

Stars now sprinkled across the dark sky. Holden wanted to enjoy the fresh air a little bit longer, so he sat down into one of the rocking chairs on the porch and just listened to the silence of the night.

The door opened and Holden watched in the dark as Olivia backed quietly out of the house and onto the porch. She set down her carryall and her suitcase, then reached up slowly to close the door behind her.

"Olivia?" he called as quietly as his deep voice would allow.

She squealed softly, like a frightened animal. Not the startled cry he'd expected, but a terrified yelp.

He was on his feet in an instant. "What's wrong?" he asked, reaching out for her.

She pulled away.

"Holden, um…I have to go home. There's an emergency."

"What kind of emergency? I'll drive you."

She shook her head, her eyes wide, the stars adding catch lights to her pupils.

"No. I'll be fine."

"Is this about…the kiss?"

"Holden, please?"

"I can't help you if you don't tell me what's wrong."

She shook her head again.

"I can't."

Holden's world felt like it was crashing down all around him.

"Livvy, what is it?"

The porch light flipped on.

Mascara streaked down her cheeks, her eyes red and swollen. She picked up her bags and ran down the stairs.

Holden followed her.

"I won't let you go," he said—feeling near the verge of tears himself. "I can't…let you go," he whispered.

"You don't understand."

"Then, help me understand," he pleaded.

"Holden?" Landon called from the doorway. He ran down the steps to where they stood. "I found this wadded up in the hallway outside Olivia's room and I thought you needed to see it." He handed Holden a crumpled photograph.

"No, please!" Olivia dropped her bags and reached for the picture.

He turned away to get a better look at the creased image, holding it up to the light emanating from the porch.

"What is this?" he asked, his brows scrunched together. "Where did it come from?"

"Lan, go get Grayson. Hurry."

His brother turned back, ran up the stairs, and let the door shut loudly behind him.

"Please," she said, "I can't put you in anymore danger."

"Danger?" The volume in his voice dialed up a notch. "Someone has been watching us, Liv. This picture was taken yesterday morning. In our backyard. While we were collecting eggs at five thirty a.m. They had to be pretty close to get a picture like this. Look at it." He held up the photograph to her face, but she refused to look.

"Don't you think I know?" The volume in her voice matched his and it surprised him. "Don't you think it scares the daylights out of me? I have lived with this nightmare for over a year. I know exactly how close he would have had to have been to take a picture like that. I know exactly how it feels to have a stranger invade your privacy, your personal space. So don't you dare lecture me on the dangers this poses. I am leaving, Holden. Before someone gets hurt. Before you get hurt."

She needs you right now.

"You're right. I'm wrong. Please forgive me." He shoved his hands in his pockets, to help him resist the urge to caress her cheek, to move the strand of hair that had fallen down into her eyes.

Her shoulders dropped. "I'm sorry, Holden." She placed her hand on his chest. "I have absolutely and unmistakably fallen for you," she shook her head, "but I can't do this." She tucked the stray hair behind her ear and bent down to retrieve the bags she had dropped.

"Say that again." Despite the seriousness of the situation, he couldn't help the glimmer of hope that displayed on his face in a hint of a smile.

"What?" she asked, shaking her head as if confused by his request.

"Tell me what you just said."

"I can't do this," she repeated. "I…"

"Not that part. The part where you said you have absolutely…and?" He waited, bobbing his head to encourage a response.

Nothing.

"Unmistakably?" he coaxed.

"Fallen in love with you. I have." Olivia dropped her gaze to the ground, then looked back at him. "That is exactly why I have to leave. Goodbye, Holden."

She made it to her car before he mustered enough courage to tell her.

"I'm in love with you, Liv!" he called out, his feet unable to stay in one place.

She froze.

He walked up behind her.

"I don't want to lose you. Please don't do this. We can handle it. Together. I'm willing to take the risk if you are." He reached out and placed a hand on her shoulder.

Slowly, she turned to face him.

"You love me?" She searched his eyes for the truth of it. "I—"

Holden closed the gap between them in one stride, wrapping his arms around her, pulling her into him, and kissing her in one swift movement. He picked her up enough that her feet no longer touched the ground, teasing her lips with his own, and spinning her in tight circles. He loved her, there was no doubt about it. She had changed him. He would be a better man because of her. She *was* his world.

CRACK.

Pain sliced through Holden's shoulder as he fell backward onto the ground with a grunt.

"Holden? Holden?" Olivia crouched down next to him.

He sat up, scooted behind the car, keeping his arm in tight to his body, and leaned up against the wheel hub. He looked down at his bleeding shoulder. There was a hole in his favorite wool-lined denim jacket. He'd been shot.

Grayson came running from the house, Landon behind him, both carrying weapons. They perched at different places on the porch, scanning the yard for their attacker.

"What's going on here, Holden?" Grayson called out across the yard. "You okay?"

"He's been shot," Olivia yelled back.

Holden pushed back his jacket and grabbed a hold of the sleeve of his red plaid shirt and ripped it loose. The bullet had just grazed the upper section of his arm, but it still hurt like the dickens.

"Wes is on his way, Hold. So are the paramedics. You hang on. You hear me?"

Holden had never heard fear in his brother's voice before. Not like this. Grayson needed to think clearly right now and couldn't be focused on him.

"Gray," he called out, "I'm all right. Are you listening to me? The bullet just grazed my shoulder." Holden glanced over toward the drive where his truck was parked and mumbled a curse under his breath.

It was too far away to safely get his rifle from inside the cab, and he couldn't risk leaving Olivia alone. He looked around, wincing as she applied pressure to his shoulder with a shirt she'd pulled from her bag. He had no idea from which direction the shot had come. For all he knew, they could be in the shooter's sites right now.

Cock-a-doodle-doo!

That evil, blessed bird.

He's over by Brewster's cage. The rooster's crow was distant, but he'd crowed all the same.

He was sure his brother had picked up on it too.

"Listen to me, Liv."

Her eyes found his and she nodded.

"We've got to get you out of here. Where are your keys?"

She held them up with a little jingle.

"Good."

His arm throbbed and tingled at the same time.

Buck up, Kane!

"I won't leave you here, Holden. Not like this."

A wailing siren mixed with the sound of barking dogs in the distance and before long the blue and red lights on top of Wes's truck illuminated the sky with color. Holden leaned back against the car and took a deep breath.

"We're going to get in the car and I am going to drive you right up to the porch where my brothers are on lookout. Keep your head low."

She responded by pushing the button on her key fob, unlocking the doors, then she handed them to him.

Holden reached up and pulled the driver's side door open, cursing the pain that shot through his upper arm and shoulder. "Go."

Olivia crawled inside and moved over to the passenger seat, then he climbed in after her. When the engine roared to life, he shifted into reverse, looked over his shoulder to make sure his brothers were out of the way, and slammed on the gas so hard that the tires squealed in protest as they spun over the gravel. He backed up, maneuvering enough so that the passenger door lined up directly in front of the porch steps.

"Get inside. Stay away from the windows. I need to know you are safe."

She leaned over and kissed him hard before pushing the door open and darting toward the front door. Holden caught Landon's eye and nodded his gratitude.

Landon acknowledged with his own nod.

Once she'd made it safely into the house. Holden shifted into a forward drive, leaning down close to the steering wheel. This time he eased his way onto the gas and slowly pulled up next to his truck. He needed that rifle. He opened his door, then, without closing it, opened the door to the truck. He reached over the seat with a groan and pulled the rifle from the back, making sure to keep as low as possible. Sweat gathered on his brow, yet he grew colder.

Several minutes passed away and there were no more shots.

Wes pulled up with Granddad in the passenger seat. As soon as his vehicle came to a stop, making a v-shape with Olivia's car and his truck, Ian gave a whistle and a command and the dogs jumped out of the back, taking off into the yard.

"Grayson said there were shots fired," Wes said, his weapon drawn.

"Holden Redbourne Kane, looks like you've gone and gotten yourself shot." Granddad said as he crouched over next to them. "You all right?"

"I'll be fine." Blood dripped down Holden's arm and onto his hand. "I think the puncture from the rooster's beak bled more." He chuckled half-heartedly. "Wes, it has been several minutes now and nothing."

"You stay here with Granddad." Wes slipped out from behind his shelter and ran in a jagged pattern across the yard to where Grayson and Landon still stood on lookout.

Holden couldn't hear the conversation, but a few minutes later, Grayson hopped the porch deck and slid across the front of the house, peeking around the corner before venturing to different sections of the yard, holding up his flashlight with his gun. Wes did the same, only he crossed the yard behind the barn to approach from a different angle.

"That's bleeding pretty good, Holden. We need to get it bandaged up or you aren't going to be any good to anyone." Granddad helped Holden out of his jacket, then ripped the rest of Holden's sleeve off of his shirt and used it to wrap around his arm. "You were lucky you had on that thick coat."

"I don't feel very lucky about now."

Granddad laughed. "Still have that dry sense of humor, I see."

After a few minutes, Grayson and Wes came back around the front of the house, their guns holstered.

Holden and Granddad both stood up and joined them at the base of the steps.

"It looks like he's gone for now, but we did find this." Wes held out a piece of cloth that had been caught in the fence of Brewster's pen." He whistled and his two beautiful black border collies came running up to him from two different sections of the yard. He held out the cloth for them to smell and they both immediately started sniffing around the grounds. Soon, one gave a howl and they both took off around the back of the homestead.

"Over here," Wes said, running after the collies.

Holden jogged after them, biting his lip as he tried to keep his arm as still as possible, every jolting impact sending a fresh piercing pain through his shoulder. The dogs didn't get far before they started circling and scratching a spot in the grass. The men looked around with their flashlights. There was no trace of the intruder.

"It doesn't make any sense. It's like he disappeared right through the ground or into the sky."

Grayson looked up at the trellis on the wall. "Not through the ground, Hold. Up the wall. He's in the house."

There had never been a better motivator for him to move so fast. Holden took off running, ignoring the pain that continued to stab at his shoulder. At least there was still feeling left in his arm.

"Don't be a hero, Holden," one of them called after him. He couldn't tell which, but he wasn't about to let some psychopath hurt Olivia. The room at the top of that trellis was hers. He burst into the house and bounded up the staircase two at a time, calling her name.

"Olivia!" he called as he approached her room. The door sat slightly ajar. Holden stood to one side, taking a deep breath.

"Please, God," Holden pleaded under his breath, "keep her safe. Don't take her from me when I've only just found her."

It didn't take long before some of the others filed up the staircase. He imagined that Landon and Wes had stayed outside to cover all of their bases.

Grayson held up two fingers, close together, and nodded as he snapped his hand toward the door.

Holden placed his fingers on the door panel and slowly pushed it open. When it had cleared five inches or so, something in the mirror at the edge of the room caught his eye. A man, dressed completely in black, hid in the space behind the door, his face obscured by a black balaclava mask.

The intruder's eyes caught his at the same time. Holden shoved open the door as hard as he could with his undamaged shoulder, gratified when it connected with their attacker. The man grunted as he was slammed into the wall, knocking the pistol loose from his grip. It slid across the floor toward the bathroom. Holden swung his rifle up into his hands and cocked it.

"I wouldn't," he warned as the man started for the gun.

The intruder raised his hands in the air and turned to face him, but before the others could get inside to help, the man reached down as he spun his body in a circular motion, pushing the barrel of Holden's rifle away from him, giving him enough time to escape.

CRACK!

The shot blew a hole in the bathroom door and shattered the mirror. The man moved with lightning speed as he slipped out of the room through the open window.

"He's gone out the window!" Holden yelled at everyone in the hallway. He darted to the open curtains and saw the man nearly half-way down the trellis. He held his rifle outside and aimed. "Stop!" he yelled.

The man looked up and caught Holden's stare, then jumped the rest of the way. Holden heard a sickening crunch as bones snapped in the man's legs when he landed, crumpling him to the ground. When the man attempted to stand, Holden shot the ground next to him and seconds later, Wes and the others had surrounded the stalker, several guns pointed directly at him.

Olivia.

He un-cocked his rifle.

"Olivia?" He called her name over and over as he stormed through the house.

Granddad stepped out of the library. "Is it safe?"

"They've got him," Holden affirmed.

Granddad held out his hand and waved his fingers in a beckoning motion. Olivia slipped her hand into his. The moment she stepped out of the room, Holden handed his gun to his grandfather, picked her up, and buried his face in her neck, never wanting to let go.

Thank you! he silently prayed. *Thank you!*

She slid down his body until her feet touched the floor. He kissed her on the mouth, his arms encircling her. "We did it," he said.

"Together."

CHAPTER TWELVE

Olivia gave Holden a quick peck on the lips.

"I have to face him," she said.

"I can understand that." He kissed the tip of her nose. "But, you don't have to do it alone." He reached down and enveloped her hands in his. "Are you ready?"

She took a deep breath and nodded.

When they got outside, Wes was helping the paramedics load a man onto a gurney at the rear of the ambulance. Olivia spotted the chains from the handcuffs and it somehow provided a sense of comfort.

It was time for her to confront her demons.

"Olivia," Grayson called as he jumped down off the tailgate of Holden's truck. He scooped her into a bear hug. "I'm so glad you are okay."

Landon joined them. He leaned down and placed a light kiss on Olivia's cheek. "Me too."

Grayson looked up at Holden. "Maybe missing dolls aren't so bad."

All three brothers hugged each other.

Wes stepped aside, allowing Olivia to approach the person who had terrorized her life over the past year. Even in the dim lighting, she would have recognized him anywhere.

"Birch Walters?" she asked incredulously. The man was the owner of a competing publishing house. She'd met him only once, but he was a well-respected member of the publishing community.

"Miss Blake," Wes said, "you know this man?"

"Yes. Don't you? He's been on the cover of several magazines and was voted most eligible businessman in Business News Today."

Olivia had believed stalkers to be lonely men who fixated on women they didn't have the nerve to talk to or interact with, not successful entrepreneurs who could have any woman they wanted.

"Hello, Olivia," Birch said with a crooked smile. "Will you please tell these gentlemen who I am? That we love each other? And that this has all been one big misunderstanding?"

"What are you talking about?" she asked. "I barely know you."

"Ah, don't be like that, darling. I know you're angry, but that will pass soon enough. It always does. Tell them there is no need for these." He lifted a cuffed hand, the metal clanking against the bars of the gurney.

"You are crazy."

"I am not crazy!" he yelled, lunging toward her, spit forming a bubble against his bottom lip. Luckily, he'd been strapped down. "You tell them!" His whole body shook as he spoke.

"Get him out of here," Holden said to Wes.

"Wait." She took another deep breath. There was something she had to say. She breathed in, then out. "You do not control me, Mr. Walters. You have no power over me and I am not afraid of you anymore. In fact, after today, I will never even have to think of you again. Until the day when my testimony will damn you to your own version of hell. Goodbye, Mr. Walters. And good riddance." She turned around and didn't look back.

"Olivia," he called.

She kept walking.

"Olivia!" he screamed.

When they got into the house, Holden slipped his arms around her. "That was very brave."

"I cannot allow that man even one more second of my life. There are too many other things I'd rather focus on."

"I hope that some of those things will include me."

"They'd better," she said with a smile. A weight had been lifted from her. She was free and ready to live each moment to the fullest.

He chuckled quietly as he lowered his head toward her. "You are an amazing woman, Olivia Blake," he said as his lips claimed hers in a kiss fraught with the intensity of a love almost lost.

She was safe in the arms of the man she loved, and right now, nothing else mattered.

EPILOGUE

Five months later

"Are you sure these are going to work?" Holden placed another tea light in a sand-filled mason jar and set it in the cardboard box on the counter next to the others. Everything was falling into place.

"Are you kidding? They're perfect." Landon twisted a length of copper wire around the rim of glass, creating a handle that would allow the lanterns to dangle from the large tree down by the lake.

Holden smiled to himself as he watched through the window as the first of three old fashioned wagons peaked over the hill on its way down to the ranch. Granddad and Olivia had thought of everything. They'd really worked hard to create an authentic experience for the group that had come for the first ever Olivia Blake Readers Retreat

"They're almost here." Holden secured the last jar inside the box and closed it up. He took it outside and placed it in the backseat of his truck, then moved to the rear of the truck, leaning with his forearms against the side panel of the bed and waited for the group to arrive.

Grayson and Olivia sat on the top bench of the front

wagon. When they reached the barn, Holden was there to help the beautiful novelist down from her perch, her hair dangling in pigtails on either side of her head. She slid down his body, her arms encircling his neck.

He placed a light kiss on her lips before setting her feet on the ground.

"Awww…" The women in the back of Gray's wagon sang in unison as they climbed down, their shopping bags and boxes in tow, with the help of his brothers and several of his cousins who'd agreed to come and help.

Holden chuckled, his gaze focused on Olivia. "Aren't you a sight for sore eyes?" he said with a wink.

"It's only been a couple of hours," she mocked with a giggle, beaming up at him.

"Long enough." He smiled and kissed her again before releasing his hold. "I still have some work to do, but I'll be back before supper."

She bit her lip and turned away, walking toward the porch. She glanced over her shoulder, her smile widening into a grin, and waved.

Ah, I love that woman.

After they'd spent the morning rounding up livestock and driving them into the fall pastures situated closer to the homestead, Olivia's guests had taken their retreat into Silver Falls for the annual Peach Harvest Festival. It was all falling into Holden's plans rather nicely.

He'd come back to the ranch to finish a few last details. Now, while the guests were playing a few pre-supper games like horseshoes and checkers, he would have time to get everything set up just right.

"Well, let's go," Landon said with a pat on his shoulder as he slid past him and climbed into the passenger side of his truck.

Holden tapped the bed panel and exhaled loudly. "Just a few more hours."

"You done good, Livvy," Ian said with purposeful poor grammar as he wrapped his arm around Olivia's shoulders as they sat on the top step of the porch.

"Isn't it wonderful?" She glanced out over the yard full of women who had become her friends over the last couple of days. They'd spent nearly every waking hour together and had gotten to know each other better than she could have ever imagined.

A light breeze blew through her hair and she inhaled the fresh air. Her hand raised to her heart as if the motion would stop it from leaping from her chest. How had she gotten so lucky to have such a wonderful reader support system?

"Thank you, Ian. For all of this." She paused. "For everything."

He kissed the top of her head and stood up. "We make a good team," he said as he stepped up onto the porch and disappeared through the back door.

That we do. She smiled.

They'd spent months planning the perfect event. Ian had commissioned three old-fashioned buckboards and a covered chuck wagon with the notion it would encourage an authentic Old West experience. He was right. Several specialists had also been brought on as independent contractors who had taught the group how to bake bread and churn butter, how to wash and hang clothes on a line, as well as providing classes on whittling, darning, and painting—all using only nineteenth century tools and equipment.

Holden had drawn up some remarkable plans on renovating barn space and the extra bunkhouse into guest suites, and had somehow convinced his brothers and cousins to come and participate in the retreat.

These good-looking cowboys had been the perfect addition as they personified everything the Blackwood family from her novels represented—integrity, gentlemanly behavior, and fun. They were really fun. And they did an amazing job teaching the ladies how to ride, to milk cows, collect eggs—no Brewster incidents this time, thank heaven—how to break wild horses, fix downed fences, start fires without matches, and to cook delicious Dutch oven meals. They'd gone out of their way to make each of her attendees feel special.

DING. CLANG. DING. CLANG. DING.

She jumped—the dinner bell.

"A penny for your thoughts." The familiar voice sent gooseflesh spiraling down her arms and back.

Holden crawled up the steps and turned to sit next to her.

"You said you would be back before supper. Cutting it kind of close, aren't you?"

Holden laughed, leaning in for a kiss.

"You two lovebirds should go on down to the lake and have a little picnic." Ian handed Holden a basket and motioned toward the garden path.

The sun had started its descent behind the mountains, the colors in the sky growing more vibrant with every minute that passed. Olivia was torn. A few minutes alone with Holden walking down a secluded path and sharing a meal with him as they watched the beautiful sunset reflecting off the lake sounded utterly delightful, but alas, she had guests to attend to.

"That's sounds wonderful, but—"

"Look at them, Livvy," Ian instructed as if understanding her reservations. "I don't think they'll notice if you're gone for half an hour."

The men in Holden's family had laid out picnic blankets all over the yard. Wes and Micah had several of the ladies laughing in line as Tad dished up their chuck wagon meals, and Grayson had already joined a small group of women who'd taken their seats at the picnic table under the oak tree.

"All right," she said with a conspiratorial smile. "Half an hour."

Holden jumped up, draped the basket over his arm, and reached down for her.

She slipped her hand into his and they jogged down the side of the yard, over the irrigation bridge, and down the path to the lake. Once the trees obscured their view from the others, they slowed to a walk, laughing.

When they reached the clearing, Olivia looked up to find dozens of little lanterns hanging in the enormous old oak at the edge of the lake. A blanket had already been laid out beneath the tree.

"You planned this," Olivia accused playfully.

"I've hardly had five minutes alone with you since you got back and I've missed you. Can you blame a guy?"

She laughed again. Commuting back and forth between Silver Falls and Denver had been hard on the both of them and, now that the retreat was coming to a close, she was looking forward to spending more time with him.

Holden set the picnic basket on the blanket. "I have to give you credit," he said as he flipped open the top and pulled out a bottle of her favorite sparkling Blueberry Apple Cider, setting it on the ground next to two fluted glasses. "For a group of romance reading fangirls, they're…not half bad."

Liv laughed. "I can't believe it's almost over."

"I think it's only just the beginning." Holden pulled out a book and handed it to her.

It was a copy of *The Rancher's Proposal*, the newest novel in her Blackwood series. Strands of heavy natural jute cord had been wrapped around the book and tied in a bow.

"How did you…" She searched his eyes. This was the first time she'd seen it complete with the finalized cover art. She narrowed her eyes at him. How had he gotten a copy before her?

"Open it," he encouraged, squeezing her hands.

She slid the string from around the book and with trembling hands she opened the front cover to the title page. *The Rancher's Proposal* stared back at her and there, embedded into the pages next to the title, was the most beautiful princess cut diamond ring Olivia had ever seen.

Holden dropped to one knee.

A spring of tears dampened the corners of her eyes, threatening to fall, but she refused to succumb.

"Olivia Blake, I love you and want you with me always. Will you marry me?"

She swallowed, not trusting herself to speak. One lone, fat tear escaped and trailed her cheek. She bit her lip and smiled.

"Yes." She nodded vigorously. "Yes. A thousand times yes," she squealed, clutching the book against her heart.

Holden stood, collected the book from her grasp, and retrieved the ring. "You..." he said as he placed the ring on her finger, "will forever have my heart." And he bent down, capturing her lips with his own in a delicious kiss that promised a lifetime of romance, of adventure, and of love.

THE END

If you enjoyed Holden's story, please consider leaving a review.

To sign up to receive Kelli Ann Morgan's new release alerts and newsletter, visit www.kelliannmorgan.com.

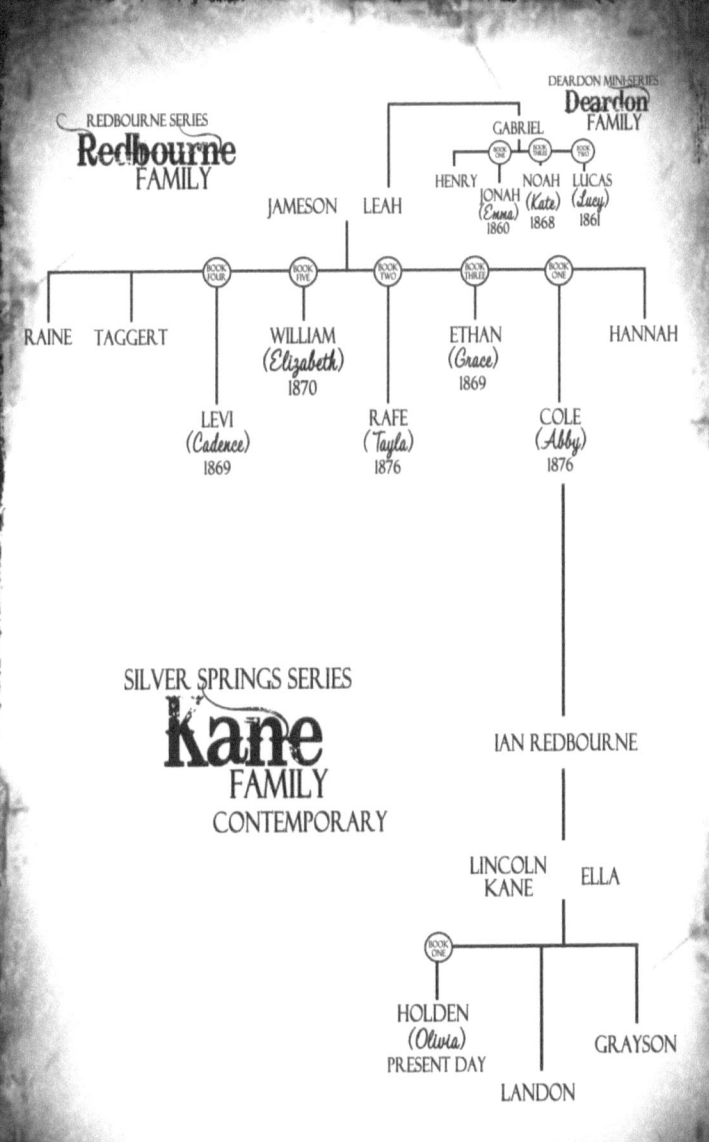

REDBOURNE SERIES
Redbourne
FAMILY

DEARDON MINI-SERIES
Deardon FAMILY

GABRIEL

BOOK FOUR · BOOK FIVE · BOOK SIX

HENRY
JONAH
(*Emma*)
1860
NOAH
(*Kate*)
1868
LUCAS
(*Lucy*)
1861

JAMESON   LEAH

BOOK FOUR   BOOK FIVE   BOOK TWO   BOOK THREE   BOOK ONE

RAINE   TAGGERT   WILLIAM
(*Elizabeth*)
1870
ETHAN
(*Grace*)
1869
HANNAH

LEVI
(*Cadence*)
1869
RAFE
(*Tayla*)
1876
COLE
(*Abby*)
1876

SILVER SPRINGS SERIES
kane
FAMILY
CONTEMPORARY

IAN REDBOURNE

LINCOLN
KANE   ELLA

BOOK ONE

HOLDEN
(*Olivia*)
PRESENT DAY

LANDON

GRAYSON

ABOUT THE AUTHOR

KELLI ANN MORGAN is a bestselling author whose western historical romance books have been downloaded over a quarter of a million times and maintain a better than four-star rating.

Kelli Ann lives in beautiful Northern Utah with her wonderfully creative and witty husband, her fun and imaginative teenage son, and two very playful cats. Before she started writing historical western romance, she worked as a photographer, jewelry designer, motivational speaker, corporate trainer and many other things, but has found fulfillment in living her dream of writing romance and designing book covers for herself and other authors.

She's passionate about creating stories with handsome, chivalrous men, intelligent, strong women, and in a world where there is always a happily-ever-after. Her novels are highly romantic and on the sensual side of PG—without all the graphic love scenes.

If you would like to receive new release alerts from Kelli Ann, please visit her website at http://www.kelliannmorgan.com where you can sign up for her newsletter.

FACEBOOK:
https://www.facebook.com/KelliAnnMorganAuthor

E-MAIL:
kelliann@kelliannmorgan.com

NEWSLETTER SIGN UP:
http://bit.ly/1iFvvwy

WATCH FOR

Landon's Love

SILVER SPRINGS MINI-SERIES, BOOK TWO